IN THE SHADOWS

A collection of works

by

Bradley H. Sinor

In the Shadows
Bradley H. Sinor
First Edition Copyright © Bradley H. Sinor, 2002
Second Edition Copyright © Bradley H. Sinor, 2016

Published by Yard Dog Press at Create Space

ISBN 978-1-937105-88-4
In the Shadows
Second Edition Copyright © Bradley H. Sinor, 2016

"Oaths" © 1996 by Bradley H. Sinor first appeared in *THE TIME OF THE VAMPIRES*, edited by P.N. Elrod & Martin H. Greenberg, **DAW** books, 1996.

"Hunt" © 1998 by Bradley H. Sinor first appeared in *HORRORS! 365 Scary Stories*, edited by Dzlemianowicz, Weinbeg, and Greenberg, **BARNES AND NOBLE** books.

"A Small Matter" © 1999 by Bradley H. Sinor first appeared in *Yard Dog, the Magazine*, Issue #23, edited by Selina Rosen, **YARD DOG PRESS**, Nov/Dec, 1999.

"Central Park" © 1999 by Bradley H. Sinor first appeared in *MERLIN*, edited by Martin H. Greenberg, **DAW** books, Sept. 1999.

"Fireflies" © 2001 by Bradley H. Sinor first appeared in *Single White Vampire Seeks Same*, edited by Martin H. Greenberg and Brittiany A Koren, **DAW** books, Jan 2001.

"Final Score" ©)2000 by Bradley H. Sinor first appeared in *Warrior Fantastic*, edited by Martin H Greenberg and John Helfers, **DAW** Books, Dec 2000.

Yard Dog Press
710 W. Redbud Lane
Alma, AR 72921-7247

http://www.yarddogpress.com

Edited by Selina Rosen
Copy Editor & Technical Editor Lynn Rosen
Cover art by Tania Mears

Printed in the United States of America
0 9 8 7 6 5 4 3 2 1

For PAT "P.N." ELROD a very special lady,
a good friend, one heck of a fine writer.

and, as always, to my Lady, my Love, Sue.

TABLE OF CONTENTS

INTRODUCTION

Since the first tales were told around a roaring campfire people have endlessly speculated on what lurked beyond the light, in the shadows. Always in those shadows have been vampires. Every culture has had its own version of these dark figures that walk beyond death.

Draw near now, my friends, and we will speak of them.

Bradley H. Sinor

OATHS

"SO you were the ones," Ryan DuLane said.

"Not entirely, but I suppose I did my share. It was more a matter of what had to be done at that moment than anything else,' said Brother Ellis.

"Isn't that always the way, Brother?" DuLane hoped that the distaste that he had for most religious types echoed in his voice.

Normally he would have barely even spoken to the monk, not to be deliberately uncivil but simply out of preference. Over the years DuLane had come to be highly selective about who he spent time with, and religious types were not high among his preferred company. There were exceptions but this monk was not one of them.

Tonight, however, he seemed to have little choice in the matter if he wanted company of any sort. The few other patrons of the Inn of the Crossed Scabbards had long since sought their beds, leaving DuLane and Brother Ellis alone in the large common room.

Located at the intersection of two growing trade routes, the Crossed Scabbards did a brisk business most the year. But spring wasn't due for another four weeks, at least, and six days of freezing rain had kept away all but the most hardy of travelers.

An hour's ride west of the inn, DuLane had come across the remains of a bandit ambush. Three ragged bodies, covered with blood and mud, lay where they had fallen. But they had not been the only casualties. Nearby there had been two quickly made cairns and crude crosses, the last resting places he learned later of several of Brother Ellis's companions.

In spite of the roaring fire, the cold and dismal atmosphere that had settled over the countryside seemed to have penetrated even inside the tavern. They could hear the wind howling outside and the rolling crash of thunder.

"However I may have performed with my sword, the bandits took two of our numbers with them," said the monk.

"But you did survive, Brother Ellis, much to your credit. From the looks of those three wretches, that would have been no easy task. Besides, I learned a long time ago, it is survival that matters. I'm just surprised you didn't bury them, it would have been the Christian thing to do"

"Survival, yes, a good thing. But even so we did not come through unscathed. Given our own wounds, myself and the others felt it best that we see to our own dead and ourselves.

"The one of our guards who lived required a dozen stitches to close up the wound in his leg. If it escapes infection he will need at least a month to recuperate." DuLane caught himself studying the monk; his tonsured hair streaked with gray only added to the lean and wolf-like appearance of his face.

"Still, you don't often associate a religious man with a sword," DuLane said lightly.

"Before God called me to the church, I found I had a small talent with the blade. It has been our Lord's will, as well as my superior's in the order, that I keep that talent sharp; in the service of God of course, rather than temporal princes. God needs many skills in his service, Captain DuLane. Yes, your name was not unfamiliar to me," said Brother Ellis.

"Indeed? To you personally, or to the Inquisition?" DuLane didn't know what the monk was looking for, but all he would find would be a man who had lived through too many battles, lost too many comrades and could barely remember what having a home and family were like.

The monk arched an eyebrow, the barest hint of a smile touching his face. "Both. I serve the church as God would have me, protecting it against heretics and those who would work against His Holy will."

"And which am I?"

"As are all men, a little bit of both. There have been incidents regarding you that have come to the Church's attention, it is true, but nothing to make the Holy Inquisition consider you a heretic...yet."

"I'm so very glad to hear that." DuLane ran his finger around the edge of his cup, collecting a few drops of wine.

"You are traveling early in the season, Captain. It must be a matter of the gravest import for you to risk the weather," he said.

Trying to be diplomatic, but still find out things, are we? observed DuLane to himself. "Indeed I must reach Sicily by the end of March or this whole journey, as inconvenient and painful as it has been, will have been for nothing."

"Then I wish you well." The monk wanted to know more; that much was obvious. It was a minor victory to leave him hanging, but one that pleased DuLane. If asked directly, perhaps DuLane would explain, but then again perhaps not.

In his saddlebags was a letter, from his old friend Karl Lysroni in Palermo. DuLane had served with him in a half-dozen campaigns, and, and though Karl didn't know it, with his father and grandfather. Now Karl was to be married and wanted DuLane to be his best man.

"Besides, who better deserves to stand with me?" DuLane had laughed when he had read the letter.

Brother Ellis leaned back in his chair.

Just then a young woman emerged from the kitchen. She balanced a tray with two bowls and a large pitcher on it that she set in front of the two men. DuLane had barely noticed her earlier, a glimpse or two through the kitchen door. This time, however, she was standing only a few inches from him and he found himself hard pressed to believe his own eyes.

She was no more than sixteen. Her dirty blonde hair tied in a single braid and then wrapped to hug her head. The face, the figure, the mannerisms, even the voice were all as he remembered them. It was a memory as fresh as a spring breeze and oh, so very old, at the same time.

"Ginnie?" he finally managed to say, turning the two syllables into three as he spoke.

"Sir?"

"Ginnie?" he asked again.

"No, m'lord, my name is Emma."

A blanket of sadness fell across DuLane. It was the response that he would have expected, should have expected, if he had not let his heart speak.

"Have you been employed here long?" he asked.

"Near three years, sir. I was born in the village just down the road. Is there anything I can get for either of you?"

"No." DuLane waved her away. But his eyes followed her out of sight.

"You know her?" asked Brother Ellis.

"No. She just resembled someone that I knew a very long time ago. Of course it couldn't be her, she's been dead a very long time."

"If I were a musician. I would imagine that I could make a great deal of what just went on, " laughed the monk. "I imagine it would make a fine ballad, of lost love, heroic deeds and valor uncounted."

DuLane said nothing, knowing just how close to the truth the annoying monk was.

DULANE waited in a shadowed corner in the Inn's upstairs hall, where he could see but not be seen. Not that long later the monk had gone to the room where the injured guard slept, paused long enough to look in the room, then went to a separate one further down the hall.

Not a few minutes later she came, candle in hand as she went to a doorway at the far end of the hall. It led to an attic area, where he suspected she slept.

Ginnie.

Guinevere.

No! He reminded himself that her name was Emma.

Ten minutes went by before DuLane could bring himself to follow her. He paused at the door. The sound the ancient hinges made echoed loudly in his memory. In between two breaths he shifted form, becoming mist and slipping beneath the door.

A long time before, when he had discovered the ability it had been painful, but that had passed. Even now he did not know just how he could do what he did, only that he could. The first time he had shown Arthur, the king had stood slacked jawed as a peasant at a traveling carnival.

The wind outside of the attic room was enough to mask the sound from the wood taking his weight as he assumed solid form again. There were no windows, and Emma's candle had been carefully extinguished, so it was pitch dark. That was no problem for DuLane. He had been born with good night vision, since the change that had only grown better and better.

There were few things to mark it as anyone's home. A small curtained alcove protected her few bits of clothing, a broken pieces of mirror hung carefully in a niche on the wall, and a small wooden ring held a section of cloth from which needles protruded.

The girl lay beneath a blanket snuggled down into a pile of straw for warmth. It would have made more sense for her to sleep in the kitchen, near the fire, but this worked well for DuLane. She stirred as he came closer, murmuring in a dream.

DuLane knelt next to Emma.

He had not fed for nearly a week, since leaving Bordeaux. The Hunger was something that was never completely gone from him, just muted. It was something he accepted, an annoyance that he had long since learned to control.

He knew he should not have needed to feed again for another few days, but as he knelt there, DuLane felt it begin to grow.

And with the Hunger, the need for blood, there were also memories.

Sunlight playing over yellow hair.

Laughter. Silk sliding across satin.

Water flowing.

The subtle movement of a smile that reached into the depths of his heart.

"Guinevere," he whispered.

Outside he could hear the wind rushing around the eaves of the tavern.

Darkness.

Light being washed away in blood.

Pain.

Green eyes swept away in a flood of red.

Another voice rang in his mind as well, the voice of the man, the man who had been his best and truest friend.

"Swear by all that you hold sacred that you will stand for the

right. That your sword will defend women, children, and all who cannot stand for themselves."

"This I do swear."

"Then stand forth and join us at the table as our brother. Rise Sir Lancelot."

Over the years he had answered to many names, worn many faces, and now it was DuLane who opened his eyes, staring at the girl.

"Ginnie," he said. His voice a hollow echo within the storm It might be Ginnie's face but it wasn't her. That much the man who had been Lancelot du Lac knew in his heart.

She probably had never heard of Guinevere the Queen, except as a sad ballad at harvest time. DuLane forced himself to stand up, turning away from the girl's sleeping form. He could feel her blood, still pulsing just below the skin, a sweet wine that could bring him strength and touch places in him nothing else had ever touched.

He remembered the oath he had sworn that long ago day in Camlin, or as it was remembered now Camelot. On his knees before the throne, feeling the steel of Excalibur as it touched each of his shoulder in turn. The words burning into his very soul.

"Swear by all that you hold sacred that you will stand for the right. That your sword will defend women, children, and all who cannot stand for themselves."

He had broken that vow many times over the years, and as the centuries had rolled by, he knew he would again.

Only not this time. He would not touch her.

EMMA came awake with a start. She had to struggle for every breath of icy air.

The feeling that she wasn't alone filled her.

For a long time she lay unmoving, waiting. But all Emma could be certain of was that a slight mist seemed to hang in the still air near her.

It faded slowly away.

THE wind whipped through DuLane, cutting beneath his cape to his heavy fleece vest and jacket. If there was a warm spot on him, he didn't know where it was. At the moment he really didn't care. DuLane bent forward as he slid through the barn's side door. Inside he could hear the sounds of the animals murmuring. His own horse, along with its tack, was in the stall at the far end.

He cursed a small cat that brushed against his leg. The feline hissed, then vanished into the shadows. None of the horses or cattle took even the slightest notice of him.

The sound of the wind faded to a distant drone as DuLane moved among the animals. He selected a small shaggy pony, one belonging to the innkeeper, and then touched the animal between the eyes. The strength of the animal echoed in its blood. DuLane could feel his fangs sliding into place as he drank deeply from the animal

A few minutes later the Hunger had once more faded into the background. DuLane wished that the memories of Ginnie, Arthur, and all the others were so easily put away.

From the other side of the barn came a voice. His hand dropped to his sword as he listened. Singing? The barn was divided into three sections. The largest was given over to the animals, as it should have been, the other two were for storage.

DuLane recognized the words as being Latin. Some sort of hymn?

That there were plenty of empty rooms in the inn made this all the more curious, not to mention the weather being a good argument for remaining indoors. He crept close to the far wall, peering through a crack in the wood.

It was a monk, but not Brother Ellis. No, this one was younger, a teenager at best, his arms wrapped tight around himself for warmth, the singing obviously an attempt to keep himself awake. Brother Ellis had mentioned a companion, Brother Francis. Obviously this had to be him. Perhaps he was serving some sort of penance and barred from the company of others.

Prudence no doubt would have dictated that DuLane not involve himself in the monks business. But curiosity had been his downfall on more than one occasion in the past.

Shifting again to mist, he drifted into the room, coming back into human form so that he was standing just behind the monk. DuLane grabbed the man by the shoulders, his fingers grinding into hard taut muscle, as he pulled the young man to his feet in a single motion.

The two men's faces were only inches apart. DuLane reached out with his mind and seized the monk's will, freezing it before the young man was even sure what had happened to him.

"You cannot move," he commanded. The young monks face went slacked jawed, his lips hanging open as if waiting for the sounds of the next verse of the hymn to come forth. "Now then, Brother." he said stepping away from him. "I have a few questions for you."

Before DuLane could say anything else he realized that they were not alone. Hunched up in the far corner of the room was a man, bound hand and foot, not even with a blanket covering him against the cold.

"So, now I see it. You're a guard," said DuLane. "That looks like a truly dangerous fellow."

The prisoner was gray and bent, his hair matted and covered with blood and dirt. One of the man's eyes began to open, slowly, unfocussed in the dark, turning toward DuLane. "Why have you come?" the prisoner's voice was a cracked whisper. "Haven't they tormented me enough?"

"Who can say what is enough," asked DuLane. "You ask who I am. Tell me who you are."

The prisoner did not speak. DuLane repeated himself. He was reluctant to try to influence the man's mind; it seemed to be on the edge of becoming unhinged.

"If you don't know me, then it is best that I be forgotten. I only wish I had been. I don't even know me anymore."

There was something about the raspy voice that sounded like one DuLane had known, once a long time ago.

"I'm not here to hurt you," DuLane said.

"Then you are a dream, a nightmare, given to torture me. If you're not here to hurt me, then help me," he pleaded. "If nothing else, kill me."

DuLane found a water skin hanging from the guard's chair. He squeezed a palm full of liquid into his hand. Lifting the prisoner's head, he offered a few drops to him.

"Help me," the man said.

DuLane stared at him. "Why do I let myself get into things like this?" he asked no one but himself.

Turning back to Brother Francis, DuLane shook his head as he stared at the young man.

On occasion, DuLane had wondered if people he controlled this way were aware of what went on around them. Not that it mattered. A few words, a gentle push with his voice and the entire encounter would become at best a fleeting memory.

"All right monk, its time that we talked," he said. "What do you know of this man?"

The young friar seemed to have trouble finding his voice. "He is a heretic. Arrested at the order of the Bishop of Marseilles, to be handed over to the Inquisition."

"What has he done?"

"I don't know, beyond the fact that he stands accused of heresy. Brother Ellis ordered me to accompany him and the other brothers. He didn't tell me why. I didn't ask."

"I don't believe you, Brother. Even monks have their gossips and I refuse to believe that the Inquisition does not have theirs. You may not have been told it officially, but I'm sure you've overheard a thing or two." DuLane reached out and pushed with his mind, into the thoughts of the young monk.

"Y-y-y-yes...I overhead about him. He is a member of dissolved outlaw order.... monks...warrior monks. Brother Ellis thinks that he can lead us to some of their supporters here in France," he said.

An outlaw order? Now that's interesting, thought DuLane. "I've head nothing of any recent dissolvings, of any of the martial orders."

"It was a long time ago. I heard them mention the papal bull that dissolved them, the *Vox in Excedo I* had never heard of it either. Brother Ellis told me to mind my prayers and do as I was told."

DuLane arched an eyebrow at those words. He knew that document all too well. *The Vox in Excedo* had been issued by Pope Clement V to formally dissolve the *Pauperes Commilitones Christi Templique Salomonis*, the Poor Fellow-Soldiers of Christ and the Temple of Solomon. The Knights Templar. The thing was that had been more than eighty years ago.

"Are you saying he's a Templar?"

"Y-y-y-y-es. That's what Brother Ellis thinks." Even though they had been extinguished in France, chapters of the Templars had found homes in Portugal and Scotland, many of them prospering. Mayhap this unwary fellow was Templar after all.

"So who is he? Does he have a name?"

"I heard someone called him Penne. Oliver de Penne."

Penne! A chill went through DuLane. He looked over at the figure on the floor. It couldn't be! Oliver de Penne had been one of the prime instruments in the betrayal of the Templars during that dark October so many decades before. He had traded his own life and safety for those of hundreds of his brothers in the order.

"If that is who he really is, then he deserves everything that you and yours can do to him, and more."

THE engraving on the medallion was worn, but DuLane didn't have to see it to know that it showed two figures, a pair of knights seated on a single horse. Around the edge were the words, written in Latin *"Non nobis domine non nobis sed nomini tuo da gloriam."* —Not to us, Lord, not to us, but to thy name give glory.

It had been in Jerusalem, in a place where he had been called Karl Ramirez, and that some said had been built on the remains of Solomon's Temple, that DuLane had first heard those words.

There, on the hot sands of the Holy Land, in a place given over by Baldwin II, King of Jerusalem, he'd sworn the vows that made him a Templar. The others who stood there that night had little known that one of their number had stood once in Camelot and now walked the world as a vampire.

DuLane turned the medallion over and over in his hands remembering faces, voices, comrades all fallen into dust just as the order had a hundred a and fifty years after its founding. Not because there was no longer a need, but thanks to the cruel betrayal and greed of King Philip of France, the Pope and one of the Templars, himself a betrayer, whose name for DuLane and the surviving brothers stood with that of Judas Iscariot—Oliver de Penne.

DuLane had barely escaped arrest himself that 13th of October in 1307. Only chance had allowed him to escape Paris. Countless others had been arrested, many tortured and many of them sent to a fiery death at the stake.

Reverently he wrapped the medallion again, in what had once been a blood red piece of silk. The colors of the cloth were faded with the passing years, another memory struggling to hold. Then he carefully placed it deep inside his saddlebag.

With a practiced eye he checked the room one more time for anything any trace of himself he might have left behind. As so many other rooms had been when he had left the place was empty.

He thought once more of the man in the barn. Was it not such a far stretching miracle that Oliver de Penne might still be alive? Lancelot du Lac still walked the earth. Though the man was not a vampire, DuLane knew one of his own when he saw them.

If this was Oliver de Penne, the betrayer, then better to let the Inquisition have him; they would stretch out the pain far longer than DuLane might; though he was certain that none of them could enjoy it as much as he would.

Swear by all that you hold sacred that you will stand for the right. That your sword will defend women, children, all who cannot stand for themselves.

This I do swear.

Then stand forth and join us as our brother. Rise, Sir Lancelot.

For a long moment DuLane heard his own voice and he also heard Oliver de Penne's plea.

"Help me."

It would be far better to take himself away from here...now.

DuLane had no sooner stepped into the hallway than he heard the creaking of hinges just behind him. Wrapping himself in shadows, he watched a single candle pass, held by the serving girl, Emma. She moved slowly, careful to make as little noise as possible.

Once she was out of sight, DuLane found himself at crossroads. He could leave, as had been his plan, but there was gnawing inside him. He wanted to look one more time into the face of the woman that he had loved and hated so many years ago.

Again, he reminded himself that she was not Guinivere. But that did not matter.

The girl had gone straight way to the kitchen. The small candle she had carried was shrouded behind several large boxes.

"Emma?" DuLane said.

The girl turned with a start, her face white with fear. In her hand were a piece of bread and a small sliver of cheese.

"M'lord?"

"It seems we both couldn't sleep." He stepped close enough for her to se him.

"Can I get you something, m'lord?"

"No...I couldn't sleep. I was considering leaving. I have a long road ahead of me."

"Leave? In this weather? It would be hard traveling and dangerous, even for you."

He reached over to touch her cheek. The throbbing of blood, her blood, echoed like thunder to DuLane. Only the Hunger wasn't there. He had feasted too well. For now it was just a lonely echo. An echo of a love lost that he would never find again.

Ginnie! Ginnie! She had been the center that both he and Arthur had found themselves jointly moving around. It had been Morganna's curse that had rapped that golden vision that was Guinivere in blood. She then in turn had dragged him into the darkness making him into a vampire, as was she.

Together the two me that had loved her, along with Merlin, had tracked she who had once been the Queen of Camelot to a lonely castle in Scotland. There they had greed her from the curse the only way they could. DuLane could still remember the silent look of peace on her face after it was all over.

It had been Arthur who had denied Lancelot the same freedom, for reasons of his own, ones that DuLane had long suspected were a mixture of vengeance and pain and love.

The girl pulled back slightly at DuLane's touch. No doubt other patrons had approached her, with fairly obvious intentions. No doubt that with the proper persuasion she had and could be most accommodating.

"Don't worry," he told her, "I have no amorous plans for you, little Emma."

"You don't?" She sounded both puzzled and hurt, cocking her head slightly in the same way that Guinevere had the first summer he had met her.

"No," he said gently.

"You loved her? And she hurt you? Now you don't know what to do?"

This time it was DuLane who was surprised. "That's right."

"And I reminded you of her?" she smiled with the faintest bit of seduction on her face.

It occurred to DuLane that he had become something of a challenge for this village girl. "You seem much wiser than I expected," he said.

"Me?" chuckled Emma. "I'm so stupid that the local priest couldn't even properly teach me my letters. Not that he should have been trying anyway. He had other plans for me."

DuLane laughed. The sound seemed alien here in the darkness. "Even so, Emma, let me pose you a question. If you had once, a long time ago, sworn a mighty oath that bound your very heart and soul would you stand by it? Even if you were the only one who remembered it. Even if it involved doing something for someone that you hated with every fiber of your being?"

It was Emma's turn to laugh. "Oaths, binding your heart and soul? M'lord your talking words that are too much for my head. I don't know if I can tell you the things that you want to hear. Just do what is right. Perhaps we can talk about it later, upstairs where it is warmer, together."

"Perhaps, but not right now."

MIDNIGHT

Brother Francis had taken to pacing about the room. He occasionally stopped and warmed his hands in front of the brazier, though his breath still hung in the air.

"Doesn't this man ever sleep?" DuLane muttered. He'd implanted the idea, not only to forget his earlier visit, but that the young monk should sleep. The later idea seemed to be something Brother Francis was unable to do.

No time like the present, he muttered, and transformed into mist.

He was in the room in a matter of seconds, but before he could resume solid form, the outside door flew open, wind and rain rushing in with two people in its wake.

"Brother Ellis?" asked the younger monk. "What are you doing here at this hour?"

The older man had a tight grip around the arm of Emma. She followed him, struggling with every step.

"Is there a problem?" the young monk asked.

Brother Ellis looked grimly around the room, face wrinkled in disapproval, as he sniffed the air.

"We may have trouble tonight," Ellis said. "This little lost lamb was consorting with a man who was acting a bit too strange to suit me."

"You think he's a Templar, sent here to free de Penne?"

"I don't know what he is. I overheard a part of a conversation between him and that wench in the kitchen. It made me expect a visit from the man tonight, so I brought her, maybe as a bargaining point, maybe not. It never hurts to be prepared," Ellis said.

All the while de Penne hadn't stirred; he lay a huddled mass in the corner. Asleep, unconscious, or dead, observed DuLane. The last would solve a number of problems.

Leaving Emma in the hands of his young cohort Brother Ellis walked over to de Penne. "You are in a great deal of trouble, my friend. You will speak, have no doubt about that." DuLane found himself wondering if Ellis was addressing de Penne or him.

"You can not escape God's justice. Like your grandfather, you will help us to exterminate this vile plague of the Temple."

Grandfather? Now that was interesting. It would explain a few things. It was far easier to believe that this was the same de Penne that DuLane had known. But it didn't really matter who he was; it had never really mattered. DuLane had simply forgotten that. In his mind he saw the Templar medallion that he had hung around his neck. *"Non nobis domine non nobis sed nomini tuo da gloriam."* —Not to us, Lord, not to us, but to thy name give glory.

Shifting his insubstantial self as close as possible to Brother Francis, DuLane took solid form again.

This time his hand was knotted into a fist and hurling toward the monk. It connected with the man's chin, the impact staggering the monk. That was long enough for DuLane to hit him again. The monk went down with a most satisfying thud.

Brother Ellis turned, rising as he moved; a sword that DuLane hadn't noticed leaped from the sheath around the man's robes. Ellis was fast, far faster than DuLane might have expected, moving with a speed that he did not hesitate to use to his own advantage.

DuLane's own sword came free, he moved to one side at the same time, feeling rather than seeing his opponent's blade pass within inches of his body. There was a not a lot of area for maneuvering in this part of the barn.

Shadows mixed with what little light there was as metal clanked against metal in the darkness.

Whatever advantage DuLane gained, the monk countered quickly as did DuLane. It seemed a contest of endurance. Then as quickly as it had begun something unexpected happened.

A cat, perhaps the same that had confronted DuLane earlier, leaped out of the rafters, screeching, to strike against his face and chest. Claws dug into flesh, hissing filled the air. DuLane twisted and tried to push the animal away.

That was enough of an opening for the monk. His sword slid through leather, cloth and fleece to drive itself hard into DuLane's flesh.

Pain. DuLane managed to shove the cat off as he went down to his knees, sword falling from weakened fingers. A curse in guttural French managed to escape his lips.

"I don't know who you are, Templar, bandit or hired assassin, and frankly I don't care," the monk said.

Ellis pulled his sword free. DuLane watched his blood follow it, leaving a dark stain on his tunic vest and a trail of dots across his clothing and onto the floor. At least he had the style not to rub thing in and clean it with my own clothes, DuLane observed.

The pain in his chest had already begun to fade. DuLane knew that deep within him torn muscles, broken veins, and ripped cartilage had begun a tedious route to mending themselves.

"Aren't you going to give me Last Rites?" asked DuLane.

"I'm a monk, not a priest. Sometimes I think you heretics would have trouble telling your right hand from your left," said the monk.

"Then brother, hear my confession while there is still time," he said.

"Very well," Brother Ellis knelt beside DuLane. "Are you prepared to confess your sins, renounce your heresy and free yourself of sin in the sight of God?"

"I am." DuLane's voice was a raspy whisper.

"Then I will hear your confession, my son."

DuLane managed a faint smile. "Thank you, brother. My confession is...I don't like you."

His hand shot up and grabbed the monk's robe. DuLane's leg trembled under him as he struggled to his feet. Holding the other man at arm's length, DuLane felt the battle rage filling him.

"I could prolong this," he said. "At another time I might have, but not now."

Wit that he slammed the monk hard against his knee. The sound of bones breaking filled the barn. From the cross beams above them came the satisfied sound of an owl's hoot.

Brother Ellis tried to say something, but blood filled his lips and then he went limp.

Through the whole scene Emma had stood quietly against the wall. Her face was a mask of confusion.

"What are you? A demon?" she asked.

"Just a man," DuLane answered. "A man who has had to do things that you might not understand because he was a man and had pledged himself and his honor."

She stepped closer, looking at his chest. The dark patch of blood had grown bigger. "We've got to get a doctor to stitch that together or you'll die."

"I hardly think that is what I need."

Emma held her hand out to him DuLane took it, his fingers gently wrapping around her wrist.

As his lips touched her skin, it was the sweetest wine that Lancelot had tasted in nearly eight centuries.

HUNT

SHE was perfect for him.

Malcolm had slipped the bartender at Dangerous a twenty for her name, Charlotte. *Uptown* and *slumming* had been his words.

Perfect.

Dangerous was a pseudo-S&M club on Manhattan's West Side; plenty of leather, whips, bare skin, and innuendo. The clientele was upscale, uptown. The kind that liked to flirt with kinky, but that was all; anybody serious about it hung out at the Corinthian, near the Village.

Malcolm turned away for just a moment. When he looked back the girl's table was empty. He caught a glimpse of her near the club's front door.

"Damn!"

There was other prey in the club, at least twenty likely possibilities. If not them, then he had his choice of the neon and lace dressed hookers that were never far away in New York.

Damnit, he wanted *her!*

It took nearly twenty minutes of prowling the streets and alleys near the club to spot her, exchanging a wad of bills for a small plastic bag.

Not bad. He'd be able to feed and get a little blow in the process.

Malcolm resisted the temptation to grab Charlotte right then. Instead, he hung back, following her. The creaking of a door far back in a nearby alley told Malcolm that a long-closed disco had a new customer.

Charlotte was sitting cross-legged in the center of the dance floor, a mirror, razor blade, rolled-up dollar bill and the baggy in front of her.

"Looks like fun," Malcolm said. His tongue traced the edges of his canines as they slid into place.

He touched her with his mind, making whatever she was, had been or could be, his.

Charlotte stretched out on the floor, vacant-eyed, a semi sensuous smile on her lips, and reached out for him. Every sound, except for the drumbeat of her heart, had vanished.

Malcolm kissed her gently, fingers trailing along the edge of her face, his fangs touching her bare neck ever so gently.

A moment later Malcolm felt himself being yanked upward and then slammed hard against the floor. Three blurry figures emerged from the darkness, pinning his arms and legs.

"This time I get the fangs!" one of them laughed.

"We'll discuss that later."

"Let's do him!"

"Let me have the honor," Charlotte said. A glowing demon of anger and hatred filled her eyes. One of the others offered her a three-foot long wooden stake, sharpened to a razor point.

The stake pressed hard against Malcolm's bare skin.

Malcolm's head jerked backward as the virtual reality goggles were dragged off his head. The transition from the darkness of the simulation to the glare of the Family training area was unnerving enough to make him grab for the platform railing to keep from falling.

Around him a half dozen other identical platforms were all occupied by others, like him, newborn vampires, each moving in their own silent training dance.

"You are dead! The true death, a rotting piece of meat in a rat infested tenement!"

A thin man with a walking stick and cold blue eyes, Malcolm's VR goggles in his hand, stared at the young vampire.

Xavier Coldsmith.

Artist.

Warrior.

Mystic.

It was into his hands that Malcolm, along with all newly created vampires, were given, to master the skills that a member of the Family needed to survive.

"I guess I didn't do too well."

"Do you think?"

Malcolm found himself wishing that Coldsmith would scream at him; that he could understand, even deal with. Instead, Coldsmith's quietly cultured voice sent shivers up his spine, making Malcolm feel like a small child who had just shown a bad report card to his father.

"I know I made mistakes."

"That's an understatement. Remember, look and then think about what you see; expect a trap, be on the lookout for it, see the partner before he sees you.

"If you can't then it would probably be better if you just picked yourself out a park bench and waited for the sunrise," said Coldsmith. "Do you want to Hunt?"

The words burned in Malcolm's ear. Since the night, eight weeks before, when he had become a vampire, Malcolm had been allowed to Hunt only twice.

The memory of those times was still fresh, better than any drug that Malcolm had ever encountered.

Only twice. Every other time he had fed, it had been from the supplies procured by the Family. It wasn't the same. And if he didn't pass Coldsmith's muster he would never be allowed to Hunt.

"Do you want to Hunt?" Coldsmith asked again.

Malcolm moved two dials on the VR controls, increasing the simulation difficulty level.

Coldsmith nodded. "Twenty per cent higher, good. Just don't get cocky, kid."

A SMALL MATTER

"I don't believe this."

"What are you talking about? Have you been hacking into the wrong computers again?"

"Wrong or right, you better take a look at what I've got up on the screen. This is a triple/triple-encrypted file I found in the Walter Reed Hospital computer network. It uses algorithms that I have never seen before. Hell, I never even thought something like this was possible."

"And you were able to break the encryption code?"

"Don't be insulting! Of course I could break it. Hell, I figured it was just the standard sort of junk the Pentagon loves to hide. You know, the 700 dollar toilet seats, international banking conspiracies, UFO research, that sort of thing."

"It wasn't?"

"You read it and tell me."

"YOU are certain of this, Xavier?"

The man called Xavier leaned the edge of his silver headed cane against the windowsill. He had been staring out at the city, forty stories below, watching the lights of the theatrical district alive with color and abounding in dreams

Xavier turned and looked at his two oldest friends, Nigel and Karl. The three of them could have been mistaken for members of the board of directors of any Fortune 500 company, which they were, but they also led another life. Call them non-human, vampire, or Nosferatu, the three of them were the leaders of The *Family*; whose traditions stretched back into the shadows of history.

"I wish to heavens it weren't, Nigel. But it is, my own sources have verified," he said.

"When did it happen? And who did it?" asked Karl.

"It appears to have been a pure chance event, caused by one of our more unstable *cousins*." Xavier glanced at a sheaf of papers lying on a large conference table. "Floyd Caldwell was his name. It happened three nights ago, in the mountains outside of Washington. His victim was walking in the forest just after sunset. Caldwell was on him before the man's bodyguards even knew what was going on."

"So where is this Caldwell? If they question him too closely no one can be sure what he might be able to tell them. Hell, a good physical exam will tell them more than they could ever imagine," said Karl.

"Again, we seem to have been lucky. The bodyguards were slow, but not that slow. They got Caldwell off his victim, but the blood was enough to throw him into a *frenzy*," said Xavier.

The Frenzy was a potential in each vampire. That moment when the lust for blood overwhelmed every other thought and desire. A time when intelligence, experience and cunning were overwhelmed in a tide of mayhem that could rip aside the curtain of myth they each lived behind.

"I take it Caldwell went for the bodyguards."

"Yes. But they were armed with Uzi's, and literally cut him into tiny bloody pieces. The remains disintegrated quickly."

"What about the victim?"

"Alive, but very weak. The doctors are as puzzled as the other authorities; the few that have been allowed to even know this happened. It was one of their computer files that tipped us off to the whole thing.

"Before you ask, I don't know if there was an exchange of blood. But we must proceed on the assumption that there was."

"Wonderful," sighed Karl. "I can see the headline now **Dracula goes to Washington**. Here's where we become the lead story on the CBS Evening News."

"Not necessarily. If handled properly, this can be a small matter that few if any outside of present company will know about," said Xavier. "Had Caldwell lived he would not have been a proper Mentor. We must supply him with one, whether he knows it or not he is part of *The Family*."

"And if there was no blood exchange and he is not becoming one of us? What then?"

Xavier sighed. "Then I will finish what Caldwell began. But let us not dwell on the more negative aspects. I will leave tonight."

"Good evening, Mr. President."

"It's good to see you, Xavier."

"I had to come. We need to have a talk about what happened to you."

Yes, thought Xavier, *I think that he will fit in well. After all, who was going to notice another bloodsucker in Washington D.C.?*

CENTRAL PARK

THE desk clerk at his hotel had given Anthony Zane a worried look after hearing that Zane was going for a walk in Central Park.

"It is two a.m., sir. This might not be a particularly safe thing to do. Perhaps you might want to wait until the morning," the clerk had said.

"No. But thank you for your concern," Zane said. "I can take care of myself."

"Whatever you say, sir."

As he walked away Zane couldn't help but smile when he overheard a single, muttered word from the clerk.

"Tourist."

Personal safety hadn't been a problem for Anthony Zane in a very long time. Not that he felt any need for weapons, but fourteen hundred years as a solider made him prefer to err on the side of caution. Tonight, a 9 mm Browning rode in a specially made shoulder holster under his jacket and a tempered steel knife lay hidden in a wrist sheath on his left arm. It didn't hurt to take precautions.

He had barely crossed the boundaries of the park when he noticed a group of shadowy figures in the distance. For perhaps five minutes they followed him, but then moved back into the darkness in search of easier prey.

Zane drew out his pipe, filled with a new blend he had purchased from the tobacconist this afternoon, and fired it up using a wooden match. Once he was happy with the way the mixture was burning, he carefully stubbed out the blackened end of the match and dropped it into his pocket.

Standing in the center of a small stone bridge in the southwestern part of the park he could look out over a small stream, at a grassy knoll at the far end of the bridge and up at the moon; letting the sounds of the city fade, if only for a moment, into a distant murmur.

"It certainly isn't Camelot, but it does sort of remind me of that little stream about ten miles or so into the woods, near the waterfall."

"OH Lance, this place is just so lovely. It makes me want to stay here forever and listen to the sound of the stream and the birds."

Lancelot looked down at the face lying against his shoulder. He gingerly reached up and touched her cheek. The resulting smile sent a feeling of calm through him.

"Ginnie, I'm afraid if we tried to do that there would be a squad of knights out scouring the forest in a matter of hours," he said.

"But how would they know where to look? We could lose ourselves here, forget politics, forget wars, just make a life for ourselves."

"Ginnie, oh, my Ginnie, if only we could. But you and I both know that is impossible. Neither of us was raised that way. I know my best friend. If we are gone too long he will have a squad of lancers out searching for us, probably convinced that we have been murdered by bandits or taken for ransom by some rival."

"I suppose so. Arthur does tend to look on the gloomy side of things at times. But, for a few hours, before we have to go back, and I admit we do have to go back, let's just live for ourselves," she said.

Very slowly Ginnie began to loosen the cords that held her blouse in place.

ZANE knew that voice.

That he hadn't heard the speaker's approach didn't surprise him in the least. He just looked to his left at the man who was standing there. He was short, barely coming to Zane's shoulder; his iron gray hair was neatly coifed, a silver headed walking stick in his hand, his clothing though simple, had an elegant cut and an expensive air.

"Good evening, Merlin," Zane said. "As I recall, Old Crow, you were either ensconced in your tower or the catacombs or enroute to a meeting with Arthur during your tenure at Camelot.

"You never seemed to stop or even have time for a little bit of fun. So it rather surprises me that you even noticed the forest, let alone a stream."

"That's what Nimue was always telling me. She said I needed to just relax a bit," said Merlin. Memories drifted across his face, giving birth to a smile that was gone in a moment. "As if I had the time. I had a kingdom to help maintain. Not only were there dark forces of magic and evil abroad, there were political necessities, balancing acts to be walked between petty rulers, deals to be struck that would buy us a year or a month or even just a few days more of peace

"Even so I did manage to steal a few hours when I tried not to let my mind linger on the next thing on the kingdom's agenda, but on her instead,"

"Indeed?" said Zane.

"Oh, my dear Lancelot. There is a lot more to me than you ever suspected."

It had been almost a century since anyone had addressed him by the name he had been born with, Lancelot du Luc.

"Otherwise how, fourteen hundred years after the fall of Camelot, would I be standing here talking with you? In those days, had anyone suggested it, I would probably have accused them of being quite far gone in their cups."

"Of course, you were known to bend your elbow with the best of them," said Merlin. "As have many other men, whose shoes you have walked in down through the years. Or perhaps I should be addressing you by the name that you go by now. What is it?"

"As if you don't know."

"Indulge me, Lancelot."

"Zane. Anthony Zane.

"How many names have you worn, over the years, how many lives have you led?"

Zane sighed, it was his time to remember, as dozens of names, some his, some belonging to people he had known, now long dead, ran through his mind.

"Too many, I think, perhaps as many as you," he said. "After awhile one loses track. All of the names, the lives, the people become blurry, distant memories. Much the way Camelot is now, a faint distant memory of a time when things were better, for me and perhaps for the world. Maybe that's what helps me keep my sanity, if I have any left that is."

Zane noticed a group of three teenage boys approaching the bridge. They were dressed in identical jean jackets, with matching bandannas around their heads, no doubt a local gang 'uniform'. The three of them paused for a moment at the end of the bridge, half in and half out of the shadows. Zane knew predators, or would-be predators, when he saw them. Zane shifted just slightly so he could reach his gun with no problem

One of the teenagers came toward Merlin and Zane.

"Evening, don't mean to intrude on the time of two fine looking gentlemen, like yourselves," he said.

"Good evening," answered Merlin.

"Gents, let's get right to the point." At that moment the sounds of two switchblades opening came from the others. Zane was fairly sure he could see the handle of a gun shoved into one's belt. "We're collecting for our favorite charity this evening, ourselves. So why don't you two hand over your wallets, any jewelry, cell-phones, stock certificates, loose change, you know the drill. Then we'll just leave you two alone and you can get back to whatever you were doing, before I so rudely interrupted you."

"I think not," said Merlin.

"I guess we get to have a little fun, cut you up and still get all the goodies," said one of the other boys

"I'll handle this," said Zane.

"Unnecessary."

With that word Merlin came round, his walking stick raised and hit the first teenagers hard in the stomach. The young man doubled over in pain. Before the other two could do anything Merlin sketched two quick gestures in the air. All three of the would-be muggers were frozen in place.

"So what are you going to do now?" asked Zane. "Something creative, I hope, that will leave a lasting impression."

Merlin walked over to each one. First he touched their temples, then placed both his thumbs on their foreheads just above the eyes. Once he had finished with the last, they dropped their weapons and walked slowly off into the darkness

"So are they going to turn themselves in to the police?"

"Please, Lance, give me credit for more originality than that. Our young friends will have a strange and eerie tale to tell, about how they barely escaped with their lives from a horrendous monster.

"If the rumor mill, not to mention the local tabloid press, works the way I expect it, two days from now people will say that there are a half dozen such beasts prowling the park.

"After that our young friends will find themselves drawn to an occupation that is more honest and worthwhile, perhaps professional wrestling," he said.

"My compliments, Merlin," said Zane.

"Thank you. Now, as to the question of your sanity. Believe me, you are quite sane; I have no doubt about that. Only the truly insane have no worries about your sanity," said Merlin.

"You're as reassuring as some of the talk shows," said Zane.

The old magician laughed, pointing in a southwesterly direction. "I think the last time I saw you was not quite a hundred years ago. Just outside of Teddy Roosevelt's office at the Port Authority."

"You still haven't lost your ability to change the subject at the drop of a hat. Besides, Theodore's office was at City Hall, not the Port Authority," said Zane.

"Oh, yes. I suppose it was, wasn't it."

"So how did you know I was here?" asked Zane

"I have my ways."

"Come now, Merlin, I've known you far too long to let you get away with a comment like that."

Merlin reached over and touched the heavy ring on Zane's right hand. In its center were two stones, one gray and one amber, wrapped in wire. The amber one began to glow, illuminating three tiny dots of red at the center.

"Let's just say I always know when my work is near," he said

Zane stared at the ring. He needed no light to see the glow; he rarely needed light to see anything. Three tiny bits of blood: Arthur's, his own and Ginnie's; he knew they were there, where they had been for fourteen hundred years.

LANCELOT!

Merlin grabbed Lancelet's sword arm. The French knight had not even realized a weapon was in his hand.

A dozen steps away stood Arthur Pendragon. In the long months since Guinivere had fled Camelot his hair had grown grayer and the lines in his face deeper. The king's iron grip held his queen by her arms, even as she struggled to escape his hands.

Only this was not the beautiful woman who had dazzled all of Camelot. This woman, her skin white and bloodless, was snarling like a beast. In the flickering torchlight Lancelot could see the long incisor fangs and the blood that ran from them, staining her lips and face.

"Lance! Lance! Help me! You've got to help me. Arthur and Merlin are mad. They want to murder me!"

Guinivere.

The Queen.

The woman that both Lancelot and Arthur loved.

That voice, whispery and sensual, was the same one that had enchanted him and haunted his memory since the first day he had arrived at Camelot. He had seen her standing near a flower-covered lattice, supervising one of the many gardeners who worked around Camelot, and from that moment Lancelot du Luc had been in love

"No," said Merlin. "She can never be yours or Arthur's, again. If you truly want to free her it must be done my way."

Merlin held a sharpened stake of hawthorn wood, three feet long, in his left hand. Lancelot looked at it, Ginnie and then at his best friend.

Arthur nodded.

Merlin moved toward Guinivere.

YOU know I wanted to die that night, the night we killed her. And I should have as well. One vampire died that night; killing a second one would have been no problem," he said

"Even after she had ripped your very soul to shreds and made you a creature of the night, you still loved her," said Merlin.

"Of course. One's heart knows little of the real world, of political realities, of dabbling among the shadows and the light. Yes, she made me into a vampire, Nosferatu, a blood drinker, a creature of the night. But that doesn't change the way I felt about her, even to the end."

"I know, and she would have approved of what I did for her and for you. Thanks to my arts I gave you back the day, and helped to add to the strength within yourself to fight the Beast that consumed her," he said.

"Yes, but why did it have to be with *her* blood?"

"And your own. It was that blood and the love that you had for her, she for you and Arthur for both of you that gave you back some measure of your humanity."

"Humanity? Was that what it gave me, or an eternity of punishment, full of recriminations and pain?"

"We had no choice in the matter, Lance, no choice at all. I needed you, Arthur needed you, the kingdom needed you, to help hold it together, they needed a hero and that is what you were and are my friend, a hero, nothing more, nothing less," said Merlin.

"So what did me being this hero get us, the table broken, Camelot fallen, Arthur dead and every bit of good we had done lost to the winds of history. What did it accomplish? To most people now Camelot is an hour and a half in a dark room with pretty pictures flashing on the screen, a book of tall tales or a bunch of people prancing about on the stage singing.

"As for me being a hero? Now, that's a laugh. I fought to stay alive, to hold the Hunger at bay. I wasn't always that successful, when the Hunger comes over me it's more beast than solider that my foes faced," said Zane.

"Lancelot, Lancelot, after all these centuries, you are still tend to feel sorry for yourself at the drop of a hat," Merlin said. "I suspect that if I could change one thing about you it would be that."

"Lancelot."

The chill that went through Zane was as cold as the grave. It was not the familiar voice of Merlin.

He turned toward the figure standing next to him. It wasn't Merlin, the magician was nowhere to be seen, he had been replaced by a tall lean figure dressed in chain mail, a rough woolen cape around his shoulders, a familiar long sword hanging at his side.

Arturius Rex. Arthur Pendragon.

"Remember, as long as you live, no matter where you go, everything that we have believed in, fought for, died for, will continue. As long as you live, Camelot lives."

"My liege, I am not worthy of the trust that you placed in me."

"You are worthy, my brother. You have proved it many times over the years, and will continue to do it."

Then Merlin stood at Zane's side once again. "He knew this road would not be easy for you. That's what made him such a good commander and king for so long."

"But not for long enough," said Zane.

"Lance. Look, we've had this conversation before, why are you bringing it up again?"

"Maybe because you're the only one who understands me, even a little bit, Merlin. After all, how many other people are there walking the streets of New York who have stood on the same piece of land as Richard the Lionhearted and The Beatles?

"I've been struggling with the idea that all I've done has been for nothing, that no matter how much trust Arthur had in me it was for naught. I struggle and it seems to do no good.

"Plus there is the date. I think the reason I'm so despondent, is the date. Fourteen hundred years ago, this very night, I watched you drive a stake through the heart of the woman that I loved."

"You think you're the only one who loved her, Lance? Arthur loved her, it may have been an arranged marriage but he still cared for her. All of the kingdom loved her. I loved her, in my own way, like a daughter," said Merlin.

Before he could say anything else Merlin looked down at the ground.

"Well, it seems we are not alone," he chuckled.

Standing next to the magician's leg was a gray tiger-striped cat. The animal didn't appear to be afraid, it just stood looking at Zane and Merlin as if it expected to be the center of their universe. Carefully, Merlin reached down and picked the cat up. The animal studied the two men, then began to wiggle itself around until it could shove its head up under Merlin's chin and begin to rub.

"I think you've made a new friend," said Zane. "I'm sure you could use one."

Merlin ignored the comment, but did begin to run his hand along the cat's back.

"Lancelot! You have a problem."

"I know that, so be serious, please."

"I'm very serious, young man, and you are a young man compared to me, and don't go asking how much older than you I am, you won't get an answer. Look, given everything that has happened to you since you left Joyous Guard, I can understand that you are feeling depressed. Hell, you would be insane if you weren't, and I think we have already established the matter of your sanity.

"There have been times when I felt the same way. Like you, I have buried friend after friend, watched those I love die, the work of decades crumble away to nothing, wondered why I even bothered.

"I think what you need to bestir you from this blue mood, friend Lancelot, is a quest," said Merlin.

"A quest?"

"Yes! A quest!"

"For what, The Holy Grail? Been there, done that."

"I know, I was the one that suggested to Arthur that you and the rest of Knights be dispatched to search for it. Besides, you wouldn't need to look far for The Grail. It's in my New Orleans condo, next to one of the bird statue props from **The Maltese Falcon**."

"Then what?"

Merlin didn't say a word. Instead he shoved the cat into Zane's arms. The animal was as startled as Zane. After a second or so it attempted to scramble out of his hands, first by leaping down to the ground, then by sinking it's claws into his jacket and scrambling over his shoulder. However, Zane's hands went tight around the cat's body and held it tightly in place.

"There is your quest, Sir Lancelot du Luc!"

"Have you lost all grip on reality, man? What in the hell are you talking about?"

"Your quest is to find this cat's owner and return it to him."

"Yeah, right, some *'quest'*."

"Whoever in hell told you that all quests had to be grand things with lives and the fates of nations balanced on the edge of your blade? Did you not swear an oath to do whatever you could to help not just the greatest but the least of people who were in distress?"

"You know I did," said Zane.

"Well, this cat is too friendly to be a feral animal, so it obviously belongs to some family who is no doubt in distress at its disappearance. So there you have your quest, find that family and help them," he said.

"Why don't you just turn yourself into a cat and escort the animal home? I think that would be much simpler," said Zane.

"Lance, you've read too much T. H. White and seen too many Disney movies. You know that shape changing was never in my repertoire. So get on with it," he said.

Zane realized that he had begun to gently rub the cat behind its ears. He was about to say something to Merlin when he realized that he and the cat were alone.

"So why don't you tell me where you live?" Zane said to the cat.

A little after ten o'clock the next morning Zane had a cab drop him on West 35th street. He knew the area. A few blocks further on was the office-home of a private detective he had occasionally had dealings with.

From his pocket he produced a small piece of paper an address written on it. The cat, who rode quietly in the crook of his left arm, watched the whole thing with an air of indifference.

It had not been all that difficult a task to find the cat's owner. Covered by the animals long hair was a rather expensive collar, complete with the name of the pet shop where it had been custom made. Two phone calls and a ride across town had brought Zane and his companion here.

A minute or two after ringing the doorbell the light on the intercom came on.

"Yes, can I help you?"

"I believe that you folks are missing a cat."

"Lancelot?"

Zane froze at the sound of the name. The door came flying open, a small form barely four feet tall appeared and the cat leaped toward it.

"You're back! Mommy, Lancelot is back!"

Zane found himself looking at a young girl, he guessed her at about ten years old, long blonde hair hanging down to her waist. She clutched the cat to her chest like the long lost member of the family that it was.

"I'd say you are home," Zane said to the cat.

"She's been worried sick about that fool cat for three days," said a woman standing just behind the girl. She was the image of the girl child, 20 years later, lithe figure, long blonde hair, a knowing smile. "Hi, I'm Elaine Appleton."

"Anthony Zane. I'm just glad I was able to bring.... what was his name? Lancelot back," he said.

"Camelot just hasn't been the same without you." The girl ignored the two adults and spoke directly to the cat, who acted as if it were his due. Which, in the cat's opinion, it was.

"Camelot?" asked Zane.

"That's what she calls her playroom, where the cat sleeps. She is totally enamored of this Knights of the Round Table thing. She has a very vivid imagination," said the girl's mother. "But then, considering her name, I suspect it would be a little hard not to."

"Her name?"

"Guinivere, Ginnie for short."

Zane felt a hard lump in his throat. Yet it was good feeling, the quest had come to a very good conclusion.

"Mommy, may I show this nice man Camelot?"

"Ginnie, I think, he probably doesn't have time."

"On the contrary, I have plenty of time," Zane said. "Lady Guinivere, if your Lady mother will give permission, and would join us, I would love to see Camelot."

"Good! Then it's on to Camelot!"

A crow with gray streaks cutting across its black feathers sat on a tree branch just outside of the brownstone door. Merlin could see Lancelot through the window. He had lied about being able to shape shift but it had been a necessary lie, something to help his old friend. Teaching lessons to hardheaded warriors was not a new experience for him.

The bird lingered for a few minutes after Zane had gone inside, then leaped off into the air. Maybe it was time to take that vacation that Nimue was always nagging him about.

FIREFLIES

> **SEEKING SOMEONE SPECIAL for a 5 foot tall dark haired SWF. Enjoys long walks and runs in moonlight. Environmentalist and protector of endangered species who loves to get close to nature, the closer the better. ISO open-minded M. Stamina & imagination a plus. If the night is your time of day and the full moon calls you, give me a howl.**

Fireflies.

Yes, fireflies. That was what the lights of Manhattan reminded Miranda of, the fireflies in the bushes outside her father's house so very long ago.

She had watched them from her bedroom window on summer evenings from the time she was a little girl. They drifted in clouds across the lawn, flanked by single outsiders cutting through the darkness. So far away and yet so tantalizingly close.

You thought you could touch them, but when you reached out they were gone. If you caught one, it was gone in a moment, as well, leaving only a tiny dark husk on the palm of your hand.

Standing in Washington Square Park it felt like they were just a heartbeat away from starting their nightly dance, yet seemingly impossible to capture or even touch.

So very long ago.

Miranda drew a long drag off her unfiltered cigarette, savoring the taste of the smoke deep in her lungs. A moment later she snuffed it out in the dirt and loose pieces of wood that covered the rough surface of the waist-high brick wall where she had been standing for a half hour. The dead stub disintegrated into ashes and paper in her hand.

She had arrived half an hour early, just so she could watch the people, watch the fireflies begin their dance. Around her, people gathered in twos and threes, music and conversation mixing together as lights of the Manhattan skyline grew brighter with the vanishing sun.

Fireflies

For perhaps the hundredth time Miranda found herself questioning her own judgment. The day she had placed the ad in the Personals column of the East Village weekly, this moment had been the farthest thing from her mind. Miranda had stared at the small personal ad form for only a moment before beginning to write.

No, that day it had been anger, anger at her family in general and The Elders in specific. The day before, and the day after, the whole idea of the ad seemed silly and even a bit pathetic. Even more so when the recorded sounds in the voice mail box that the newspaper supplied began to accumulate.

Then there had been his voice.

Kyle.

Her original plan in dating a human was to do something to enrage the sanctimonious Elders of The Pack. *"Humans are Prey, nothing more, nothing less!"*

Not that she really disagreed; it was more their attitude, their demands of controlling every single aspect of her life.

She looked around her, at the street performers, the singers, the punks, the lovers, all the figures that filled the night in Washington Square. It was a scene she was quite familiar with. Even so her stomach was churning with uncertainty.

In full lupine form she could prowl in any of the five boroughs, easily taking her prey from the most deserted sections of the city. The Elders had long preached that the Pack should hunt only along the edges of humanity, through broken buildings and into the shadows of forgotten lives.

That was no challenge, no fun, and Miranda enjoyed a challenge. So, taking partially human, partially wolf form, *she* sought out *her* Prey in places like Times Square, or even on Broadway itself. During The Hunt was when Miranda felt fully alive.

The tales told by the occasional survivor, the ones she *allowed* to get away, were too fantastic for even the most lurid of tabloids to print, although some had. Miranda had kept a few clippings, headlines blazing out in 18-point bold letters:

MONSTER PREYS ON MANHATTAN
KILLER RIPS THROATS FROM VICTIMS
12-FOOT TALL BEAST
PROWLS CENTRAL PARK

The last one amused Miranda, considering the fact that even in her highest heels she stood only five foot three. Besides, she rarely went anywhere near Central Park. Someone else was responsible for that little rumor.

No, it was not fear that set her stomach churning. It dawned on her that ever since she had made the date to meet Kyle she had been worried whether she would actually like him, and vice versa. "How... human," she said softly.

The big clock on the bank switched its display over to read 9:00. Miranda felt *his* presence, a gentle shifting in the air, a change in the lights around her.

Kyle.

A tall thin figure, dressed in dark grays that seemed to flow out of light and darkness at the same time, his straw colored hair seeming to glow in the reflected lamplight that filled the park. As he passed them people stepped away, like fireflies darting away from the light.

"Good evening, Miranda, I'm Kyle," he said.

Miranda straightened her leather jacket, pushing it open to reveal her purple blouse and the silver wave-shaped belt buckle at her waist.

"And how can you be sure that I'm this Miranda you're looking for?" she said.

Kyle reached out and took her hand.

"The same way you know I am who you were waiting for," he said.

The funny thing was, if one of her cousins had described this situation to her, Miranda would have been certain they had OD'd on too many designer drugs and far too many romance novels.

Miranda had the sudden feeling that this was going to be a very interesting evening. Okay, he wasn't exactly what she had expected when she placed the ad, and they had talked. He was better. Showing up with him at Pack functions would be sure to enrage the Elders; she could almost hear most of the females in the Pack drooling over him now. All this was going to really help twisting the knife in the Elders' collective craw.

But there was something *different* about him. Different, but familiar. Miranda couldn't quite put her finger on just what it was, but there was something. Deep inside her The Beast recognized that difference in Kyle, and was howling in agitation. It would be so simple to let herself go, let the Beast have its freedom. But no, not now, not now!

"You can still walk away," he said, as if sensing her uncertainty.

"True. But so can you. And given the circumstances, I wouldn't blame you in the slightest," she said.

"I wouldn't dream of it," he said.

"Neither would I."

FROM beyond the borders of light formed by the flickering tiki torches that marked the edge of Kyle's rooftop balcony she could hear the screeching of police sirens. Rescue trucks and ambulances filled the night, all seemingly headed in the same direction. She wondered what was going on. First one sound, than two, then three, until there were too many to pick out individual ones. Miranda followed the sounds, listening to them merge, separate and then fade away.

Disappearing, like fireflies with the coming of light.

Fireflies.

"Here we go," said Kyle.

The sound of his voice gave Miranda a start. He moved quietly toward her, carrying two brandy glasses. It bothered her that she had not heard him approach. There was that dammed feeling again, *something* that she could almost put her finger on, but not quite. If it were something Kyle was deliberately hiding, she had to admit he was good.

She savored the aroma of the amber liquid for a long moment before letting a tiny amount slip across her lips. The taste was a thick, heady one that both burned and exhilarated as it rolled down her throat.

"This is old and very good," she said. "I'd say it was not from this century."

"And I would say that you are quite right," said Kyle. "You have an exceptional palette for one so young. It was laid down for one of Napoleon's Marshall's."

"Marshal Davout, or perhaps Soulet? I doubt it was Massena, he was too much of a teetotaler"

Kyle arched an eyebrow at her. He was startled and that was exactly what Miranda wanted. After all, you don't expect a blind date to be able to spout off the names of some of the Marshals of France under Napoleon Bonaparte.

"So, did you slip an aphrodisiac in it?"

"Do I need one?"

Miranda laughed.

This evening had definitely *not* been the sort of thing she had expected. For a few hours she had been able to relax, to forget who she was, and to be just Miranda. She realized that it had been a long, long time since she had been able to do that. Just be Miranda. Not Miranda du Shane, daughter of Conrad and Esther du Shane; not Miranda, a daughter of the Pack; not Miranda, a were who stood outside of humanity. Just Miranda.

They had walked and talked for what seemed like hours. Eventually Kyle had led them to a small club in the East Village, Greely's Pub.

"I think you are going to like this place," said Kyle. It was decorated in the style of any number of pubs that Miranda had seen in Ireland and Scotland. But without the veneer of faux-Celtic that far too many of these places in New York had.

They had laughed and drunk and danced. At one point, Miranda was pulled on stage with the band and handed an Irish drum to join in their rendition of "Gypsy Rover". The musicians seemed pleased with the result, as was Miranda.

"Is there anything you aren't good at?" Kyle asked.

"Many things."

"Perhaps we can discuss this over some brandy somewhere else?"

"And where would that be?"

"At my apartment."

They sat and sipped their drinks, listening to the sounds of the city around them, feeling the breeze as it moved across the patio. Their eyes locked and everything around them faded away. Then, between one heartbeat and the next, lips, tongues and hands began to probe every inch of their bodies, moving faster and faster across clothing and then bare skin.

Kyle lifted Miranda, holding her in the air, her long legs wrapped around him. Miranda's nails shifted to claws, carving deep paths across Kyle's back, trails of blood marking the places she had touched.

"Oh don't they just look so purrrrty!"

"Yes, its just pure dee romantic, like one of those movies with Tommy Hanks playing him, and she'll be played by little Meggie Ryan."

"Yeah, the gigolo and the bitch!"

Miranda had come awake a moment before the first one spoke. She and Kyle had fallen asleep on the futon. It was just after 2:00 and they were no longer alone.

Three figures stood near them, relaxed and watching. She didn't even have to see them clearly to know they were there and who they were, their scents were quite familiar. *Pack!* Gregory, Dean and Michael Ray; her cousins.

She opened her eyes, muscles tense and ready to react, and slowly rose on one elbow. Her relatives had not chosen to come in full wolf form; instead they wore the part human, part lupine appearance that had occasionally graced the covers of such intellectual publications as the Weekly World News.

Deep inside her the Beast screeched, demanding to challenge them. Miranda smiled. This wouldn't be the first time that she had had to put them in their places. It wouldn't be the last, she knew that much.

"Should I ask something stupid, like 'What do you want?'" said Kyle.

Miranda looked down at her lover. He had not moved a muscle, his breathing hadn't changed, nothing to alert her to the fact that he was awake. His voice was calm and unemotional.

"I suppose you could," said Gregory. His small narrow figure was half hidden behind a large container-grown tree.

"If it makes you feel better," said Dean. "You can say any damn thing that you want and I certainly won't stop you."

"Of course," said Miranda's other cousin, "That doesn't mean we might not do something after you've had your say."

"Thank you. I wondered when you three idiots were going to show yourselves. I've known you were following us since just outside of Washington Square. You might as well have been carrying signs."

Before the last word was completely spoken Kyle was on his feet. He moved with a speed that surprised Miranda, grabbing Dean and throwing him hard against the balcony wall. He stood there, stunned, a moment and then slid to his knees, surprised and disoriented, the breath knocked out of him, but otherwise unharmed.

Kyle turned on one foot to face the nearest one, Dean. Then, suddenly Kyle was gone. He had leaped ten feet straight into the air and came smashing down into the other man's back and sent him into a heap on the floor.

"Good, you're good!" said Michael Raye. "But I'm better!"

"Fight, don't talk, puppy," said Kyle.

That was when Miranda caught sight of Kyle's fangs. The incisors had shifted down into place, weapons as deadly as Kyle's hands. She realized now what that *something* she had sensed about him had been. He was Family, Vampiri.

"Stop this! Stop it now!" said Miranda.

The Beast flowed over her, seizing her and beginning the change with a speed that startled even Miranda. Like her cousins, she did not take full wolf form. A fine reddish- blonde fur covering her bare skin in only seconds; the Beast voice echoing from her lips.

"I said stop it, before I tear you all apart!"

Kyle and Michael Raye did not break eye contact for nearly a minute. The other two were getting stiffly to their feet, uncertain of what to do now.

"Pack?" Kyle said, politely to Miranda. Though from the tone of his voice and look of amusement on his face she knew he had known her for what she was from the beginning.

"Well, duh! You were expecting maybe Martha Stewart? Now, all four of you back off. I'm never one to stop a fight, but this is a piece of ridiculous nonsense!"

"It's 'is fault," said Gregory " 'e started it!"

"Gregory," said Miranda. "We'll have none of that phony British accent of yours. Everybody knows you were born in Tahlequah, Oklahoma."

"Look man," said Dean. "We just wanted to put a scare into you and our little cousin. Anything else she had planned was all her idea."

"We didn't know you were Family," said Gregory.

"Look, puppy, you invaded my aerie, my home. I have every right to beat the daylights out of all three of you and tack your worthless hides up over the mantle," said Kyle.

His voice was cold and as menacing as anything that Miranda had ever heard. Far different than the man she had met a few hours ago in Washington Square. That man seemed gone now, like a firefly held in someone's hand.

Fireflies.

"Anytime, anyplace," said Gregory.

"No! If you try anything, he won't have to do any more than watch," said Miranda. "I will kick your collective keesters from here to Crabapple Cove, Maine! And you know I can do it or don't you remember what happened last July 4th, if you don't think so!"

Miranda's three cousins looked at each other, then at her. One at a time they shifted back to human form.

"All right," said Dean. "Will you be coming with us, Miranda?"

"No," she said.

A look of confusion crossed Gregory's face. "You aren't thinking of ... I don't think a member of the Family qualifies as proper Prey."

"No, he doesn't. But I'll be staying here for awhile, anyway," she said.

"You know The Law. Pack and Family do not mix. The Elders will not be happy," said Gregory.

"I don't care. I've never cared what The Elders had to say," she said. "I'll be staying. That is, if Kyle wants me to."

Kyle answered by taking her hand in his.

YOU know that the Elders, both of Pack and Family, are not going to approve," said Kyle.

Miranda nodded. "That's what I had in mind from the beginning, gaining their disapproval. I hardly intended to involve you or The Family in my little strategy," she said.

Kyle smiled, then said in a high nasal voice, with just a touch of faux-Bostonian accent. *"A vampire and a werewolf. Oh no! Simply will not do! Not at all, at all! After all, what would the other Families say?"*

That about summed things up, although her parents and cousins of The Pack would, no doubt, be a lot more vitriolic about the idea of a relationship with Kyle. It was as serious as if he were a human, a.k.a. Prey, but a different type of serious. She could hear her father's voice quoting the Law: *"Pack and Family do not mix, save under the most extraordinary of circumstances. They go their way, we go ours, and these are not extraordinary circumstances.*

"You realize that we could be Outcast."

Being Outcast was a threat as dire as any that could be made to vampire or were, short of a *Dark Hunt*, where one of their own was Prey, and which could only end in the Final Death. The Pack was the center of the universe to a were. The Pack took care of its own, as did The Family. If you were Outcast, no longer part of The Pack or The Family, then you were Prey, as surely as if you were a mortal born.

Miranda had never seen it happen. She had heard tales of The Dark Hunt. But there had never been one in her lifetime. They were things told around campfires in the depths of the night. The very idea of being cut off was nearly impossible to conceive.

"I know, and I don't care," she said. "Do you?"

"Not particularly," he said. "Uncle Xavier has always said that I would come to a bad end."

"A bad end! That's a nice thing to say to a girl!" Miranda threw her head back in mock indignation. Out of the corner of her eye Miranda thought she spied a firefly, but when she turned toward the insect, she found an owl perched on the wall, watching the whole tableau.

Without a word, she angled her head toward Kyle, offering her bare neck.

Kyle's fangs touched her like a whisper, leaving a sensation in their wake as intense as their lovemaking had been. He barely took a spoonful of blood, but she would not have begrudged him more. Freely given, there was a strength in it that did not come otherwise.

"I hope we're not interrupted by anymore of your gate-crashing relatives, said Kyle.

Miranda let out a long sigh. This was a moment that she knew would come, it was time to lay her cards on the table.

"I'm afraid that that was my fault. I sort of wanted someone to find out that I was dating outside of..."

"The Pack? Your species?" he said.

"Ah...yeah. I knew it would drive The Elders crazy. So after we made our date for tonight I made sure I let it slip to my blabbermouth sister, Linda, what I had in mind. You should have seen the look on her face when I said you weren't to be Prey," she said.

"So when did you pick up on the Rover Boys?"

"Practically from the time I got to Washington Square. You may have noticed they are about as subtle as a train wreck. I figured they would follow us and report back, not try to stage a rumble on your balcony. By now the Elders know about us. I would say they will be furious, which is exactly the way I wanted them."

"Does it matter to you, how they feel?" asked Kyle.

"Yes, but not nearly as much as it did before I placed that ad, before I came to the park."

"So what are you going to say to them, now, about us."

"Probably the same thing you'll be saying to your Uncle Xavier and the rest."

"Deal with it?"

"Exactly. I like the way you think, mister."

"Oh, really. Do you just want me for my mind?"

"No, your body as well," she said as she padded back to the futon, motioning for Kyle to join her. He moved soundlessly to her side, cupping her face in his hands and bending his head down to kiss her. His touch sent an indescribable thrill through her body.

There would be trouble ahead, and a part of her relished the possibility, but for now all her worries melted away in Kyle's presence. This whole affair may be brief, she thought as her lips met his, but like the fireflies it would burn just as bright.

FINAL SCORE

"CAN I get you something, m'lord?"

For a moment Ashe was sitting once again at his favorite table, just to the right of the door at the Bearded Cockerel Tavern. The place was a dump, the thatched roof needed patching, the rafters were cracked and burned and the ale was heavily watered, but the memory of it was as precious to Ashe as anything. That was a moment he would have given anything to make last.

"M'lord?"

As they all do, memories fade. Only this time Ashe found himself facing something *almost* as pleasant. A young woman, dressed in a dark green blouse and brown skirt of a style that would have been at home on any of the tavern wenches at the Bearded Cockerel.

He caught himself about to address her as Cassie, the name of a woman near fourteen hundred years dead. But Cassie would never have been wearing a pager on her belt and a button with the inscription **"Goes From Zero to Bitch in 4.5 Seconds."**

"I'm sorry. I let my mind wander a bit," he said.

"It's early," she smiled.

"So, what can I get for you, m'lord?" The girl was at least not trying to affect a British accent. Most of them came off sounding like something you hear on reruns of *Fawlty Towers*.

She was one of several employees in what had been dubbed The Cross-eyed Tavern; one of over two dozen refreshment tents and booths that were part of the three day long Medieval Fair staged by the University of Oklahoma.

In the twenty years since its beginnings, the Fair had outgrown its original campus site. Now it was staged at a nearby park, in the shadow of the towering gothic spires of the university's library and Owen Stadium, home of the O.U. Sooners football team.

"I don't feel like coffee this morning and it seems far too early for anything stronger," said Ashe. "With those restrictions, what would you suggest, m'lady?"

"I take it caffeine is your drug of choice?"

"Exactly."

"Well then, we do have several very good breakfast teas." She pointed toward a large chalkboard just to the right of the bar.

Ashe scanned the list. Most of them had names like King Charles Best and Queen Anne's Delight.

"Try the Prince Alfred special. It's really a variation of Earl Gray, heavy with caffeine with a very distinctive blend of cinnamon and some other things. It will definitely wake you up," she said.

"Kind of the Jolt Cola of teas?"

"Exactly!"

Ashe accepted a styrofoam cup from her. The smell was strong. He had tasted better, much better, but for the circumstance this was far better than he had expected.

The girl watched him for a moment. "Is this your first time?"

"Drinking tea?"

"No, at Med. Fair, silly?" she laughed. Ashe smiled at the sound of her laughter. It was a momentary light in the darkness.

"Yes. I've been to some in other places, but that was a long time ago."

"If you want a guide, stop by just after noon. I'll be off work then."

"Maybe," said Ashe.

"No maybe about it."

ASHE sipped on his tea as he watched the sea serpent. It wallowed from side to side in an ungainly dance, slowly cris-crossing the small man-made pond. The water was just dirty enough to hide the guide wires that were pulling it, unless someone stood on the stone bridge and watched for more than a few minutes. An odd looking section of rock next to the bridge seemed to be where the motor had been hidden.

It had been the serpent that had brought Ashe to Norman, Oklahoma, and to the Medieval Fair.

He didn't need to pull the much-folded sheet of yellow paper out of his wallet.

It featured an elaborate pen and ink rendering of a sea serpent rearing its head out of the water, the turrets of a castle in the background. Duplicates of it, blown up to poster size, had been spread out all across Norman and surrounding towns announcing the three days of the annual celebration.

He had found the flyer crumpled up in the corner of a certain cheap house in a Baltimore suburb. But knowing the occupant's obsession, it had been enough.

The serpent, at least, was an attempt at something special. Not a too successful one, especially since the rivets in its metal hide were clearly visible, but an attempt none-the-less. Ashe took another drink. The caffeine left a warm, welcome feeling in his throat.

Below him a half dozen ducks and a lone goose paddled across the pond, carefully steering clear of the serpent. It would be quite the unexpected surprise if the beast were to accidentally run down one of the birds. Ashe wouldn't have been surprised if that happened.

"You've got to be less cynical, stop expecting the worst, let yourself enjoy life a little bit more. Don't be so afraid to just live."

He could still hear her voice. Hannah Cortez. Half Spanish, half Irish and bloody proud of both sides of her heritage. When he closed his eyes he could *almost* feel her standing next to him, a gentle touch on his hand, whispered breath along the back of his neck.

"Hannah," he whispered, crushing the styrofoam cup into pieces, the remaining tepid liquid dripping between his fingers.

Ashe had met her only sixteen months before. It had been a glorious time, a time he had been happy. That any who he loved would die eventually was something he had reluctantly grown used to in the fourteen centuries since he had watched Camelot fall around him. But Hannah had not been taken as a casualty of war or as part of the natural order of things. She had been murdered cruelly, painfully, slowly.

Now, as he had when he had been a knight of Camelot, when he had been a brother of the Knight's Templar and so many other things, it fell to him to find her killer and exact justice.

Ashe let the styrofoam pieces of his cup fall into the dirt near the bridge.

THE Medieval Fair actually covered nearly ten acres. Parking fanned out along the edges of the grounds and then snaked down through the neighborhood, forming an intricate kind of spider web along the streets.

The radio had said that there was a better than fifty percent chance of rain, so he had his choice of whole rows in the parking lot. Until the weather cleared only the hardiest would venture forth. He hoped the man he was looking for would fit that description.

Ashe walked with no destination in mind. The food booths and the artisan's tents had been laid out in no obvious order or logical pattern that he could discern. Right now he just wanted to look and listen and wait.

Later in the morning Ashe stood watching a small man dressed in a vaguely medieval costume made up of the most outlandish combination of colors: purple scarf, orange shirt, a black feathered cape. The little man was deep in conversation with a fellow wearing what looked like a dark brown tuxedo jacket, jeans and no shirt.

Ashe smiled.

No doubt the two of them thought they were being outlandish, original, standing out from the crowd. He had seen it all before, more times than he could count, and each time watched the would-be rebels blending into an ocean of sameness.

"You are looking far too philosophical for your own good."

Standing almost at Ashe's elbow was the young woman who had waited on him that morning. She was smiling and had exchanged her apron for a beaded vest and matching gypsy-style headscarf.

"Really?" he said.

"Really."

"Well then, if not philosophical, how should I look?" asked Ashe

"I'm not sure," she said. "Maybe like you were having fun?"

Ashe chuckled. There was something infectious in the girl's attitude. "Hmm...fun? Now what is that?"

"Fun. F...U...N. Fun. It is definitely something that I think you should have," she said. "And I'm going to make sure you have it."

"Yes, and you can't say you weren't warned. I did tell you this morning that I would see you again."

"Well, seems you were right. If you're that good at predicting things, how are you on the lottery, or maybe the daily double at Fair Meadows Race Track," he said.

"I might be afraid if I were right and just as afraid if I were wrong," she laughed.

"A wise attitude. One that I think a lot of so-called seers would have been better for, had they adopted it," he said.

"You *are* quite the philosopher, m'lord, *quite* the philosopher. I've not heard many of the fellows around here saying things like that. They mainly speak longingly of the glories of war and the prowess they would bring to battle," she said.

Memories of battles without end danced among Ashe's memories—the pain, the stink of blood, the screams of the dying, the utter exhaustion that permeates a soldier, both in the body and soul after a battle.

"The only honor in battle is in having survived. The only glory comes in those tales told by fools and the songs sung by minstrels. A great adventure is what you have when you're telling the tale over a pint and a good meal afterwards; when it's happening you're scared out of your wits and certain that you will die in the next second, if you 're thinking at all. Anyone who isn't, is a fool, a fanatic or a fake," he said

"You certainly don't sound like the medieval reenactment guys I've been hanging around with," she said

"Each to their own. "It occurs to me, m'lady, that I have not had the honor of knowing your name."

She grinned and curtsied, almost colliding with a boy in a jester's hat. "M'lord, I am Serina de Lyman. I am most pleased to meet you."

Ashe bowed at the waist in the courtly fashion that he had been taught in Italy.

"A beautiful name for a beautiful lady. My name is Landon Ashe."

"Actually," she smiled. "My real name is Serina Smith. I added the last part for the Fair and for medieval reenactment events."

"None-the-less, it is lovely. So when do you have to be back at work?"

"By pure chance, I'm off for the rest of the afternoon."

"Pure chance, indeed? Since I'm a stranger in town myself, I'm still in need of someone to show me around the fair."

Serina grinned. "I think we can find you a guide."

"**THAT** is a most unusual stone in your ring, sir. I don't think I've ever seen one like it before."

Ashe and Serina were standing in front of the large tent of a vendor who dealt in jewelry that ranged from lost wax designs to wire wraps to what appeared to be hand made specialty designs. Serina had spotted a small necklace done in a Celtic design around the profile of a bird in flight.

Ashe nodded. The ring was unusual, the stone a piece from the Giant's Dance, and crafted by no less than Merlin.

"The man who made it was an old friend. He gave it to me for luck."

Ashe couldn't help but smile at that. Over the years he had called Merlin many things; in those first days, when Ashe had been known as Lancelot, that had actually included friend.

"And has it brought you luck, sir?" the jeweler asked.

"I suppose you could say that."

"Well, if you were inclined to part with it I have an idea it would fetch a pretty penny. The workmanship is so detailed. I'm not sure what kind of stone that is, but it is one that holds the eye." The thing was, even if Ashe wanted to he couldn't part with it, the effects, especially if he were caught out in the direct sunlight, would be most unpleasant and very painful. He did not like to recall the few times that had happened.

"So, what do you think? Is it me?" Serina held the necklace around her neck. It hung to the edge of her low cut blouse, the silver surface shining against her skin.

"It looks as if he made it with you, and only you, in mind," said Ashe.

"Oh, get off with you now," she laughed.

Serina had turned to the jeweler when Ashe felt someone grabbing his shoulder pulling him sharply around. He found himself facing a man in his early twenties, dressed in a black and white musketeer's style costume. The man's buzz cut seemed as out of place as a Grateful Dead tee shirt on a samurai.

"What the hell is going on here?" said the stranger.

"Michael! What do you want now?" yelled Serina. She obviously knew him, and just as obviously did not like him. The young man called Michael ignored her, moving at Ashe until he was only inches from the other mans' face.

"What kind of man are you, trying to put the make on my woman?"

The crowd, sensing a fight about to begin, moved back clearing a rough circle in front of the booth.

"Michael! I told you last week that we were through. You're only making a fool of yourself! What does it take to get through that thick skull of yours, a two by four?" she said.

"Shut up! I'll deal with you later!"

"If I were you, Michael," Ashe said softly. "*I* would take what the lady says to heart. And I would be wary of how I spoke with her, if *I* were you."

"Are you threatening me? You're not me and I don't need your advice!" hissed Michael. As he spoke a dagger dropped out of his sleeve into his hand.

"I'm tired of this macho bull crap!" said Serina. Instead of turning away, she jammed herself in between Ashe and Michael.

"Get out of the way, Serina," said Michael. "This is between him and me."

"Wrong answer!" Serina slammed her knee hard into Michael's crotch. His face contorted with the sudden pain, a loud groan rolling out of his mouth. The knife dropped, hitting the side of the counter before it clattered to the ground

He looked at her, pain, surprise and confusion rolling across his face. He tried to speak, but before he could Serina punched him hard in the stomach. The impact was enough to send him to his knees. Around them the crowd, who had been yelling encouragement, broke into applause.

"M'lady Serina, it's obvious you don't utter threats," Ashe said. "Remind me never to get you mad at me."

"I don't know why he can't understand that we're through and I never want to see him again," said Serina.

She and Ashe sat on a small boulder near the pond. Around them the voices that were the Medieval Fair and its participants rose and fell. Serina hadn't spoken for sometime, hadn't even looked at Ashe, just watched the ducks and the sea serpent.

It had taken less than a half hour to explain things to the off-duty police officers who were working security for the Fair. Thanks to more than a dozen witnesses, not to mention Michael's fairly long police record, Ashe and Serina had been allowed to go with no problem.

"Just because he said he was sorry after I caught him in the sack with two different women, at the same time, he thinks I should forgive him."

"Two?"

"Yeah, two," she sighed. "When I walked in on them, the asshole had the gall to suggest that I join them in their little games."

"That just proves what I already knew; Michael is an idiot."

"On that we agree." Serina grabbed Ashe and pulled him tightly to her. Their lips met in a hard passionate kiss, her hands moving up and down his back. Ashe's hands responded gripping her shoulders tightly.

"My apartment is only a couple of blocks away. Think you can show a girl a good time, mister?"

"I think I can."

"You better."

ASHE gently touched Serina's shoulders. Then he began massaging her shoulders and neck. Serina let out a long sigh as his fingers worked her muscles back and forth.

"You only have about a week to stop that," she murmured.

Ashe smiled and continued to work. Every now and again a sound would give him proof of her approval. Slowly he let his hands begin to work their way from her shoulders, first to her arms then around her breasts. He cupped one, then the other, moving in low regular motion. He began to kiss her neck and then moved gently along her shoulder.

"Oh yes," Serina murmured. She turned, facing him, pushing her breasts hard against his chest.

Ashe felt his fangs sliding into place. He touched them to her wrist, her breasts and then her neck.

"Ah, m'lady," he said softly

As he drank deeply from Serina, Ashe's hands worked swiftly, slipping her blouse off her shoulders, and then her skirt flowed to pool around her ankles. Her own hands had begun to pull Ashe's clothing off of him.

"I want you," she murmured hard into his ear.

THE party, hosted by the local chapter of the medieval reenactment organization that Serina belonged too, was being held in a loft that covered a half a city block in downtown Norman.

Serina had outfitted Ashe in a knee length tunic, soft suede boots, cape, hood and sword. The style was 10th century Welsh with a dash or two of Scottish.

"You look fantastic. It's like you were born to wear this type of clothing."

"Perhaps I did," he said. "In another lifetime, of course."

"Maybe so, m'lord," she said.

Serina had opted not for her tavern wench outfit but for a more elegant fourteenth century Spanish style gown in green and black. Ashe had noticed her slipping a few things into her belt bag that he definitely didn't remember from that time period, her pager, a roll of breath mints and a canister of pepper gas,

As Ashe and Serina made their way along the street, they spotted a man in Roman armor standing in deep conversation with a woman in a Russian style gown. Nearby a Japanese samurai was puffing on a corncob pipe.

"I think this must be the place," Ashe said to Serina.

"I wonder what could have ever given you that idea. Could it have been those two dressed so strangely?" She gestured at a couple of guys standing in front of a theater marquee across the street, wearing football jerseys and shorts.

"Exactly. They're such an anachronism when compared to normal people like us."

"I'm beginning to wonder about you, m'lord," Serina said, smiling.

"Good," said Ashe.

Serina led them up a long outside stairway. Once inside she was recognized almost at once, even as the door herald announced their arrival. "Lady Serina de Lyman and Lord Landon Ashe."

They were no more than twenty feet beyond the door when someone motioned Serina over. Ashe recognized the woman as the other person he had seen at the tavern tent that morning.

"It's my boss," Serina said. "She's supposed to have the shift schedule for the rest of the Fair."

"Go make nice," Ashe told her. "It always helps to have the boss on your side."

"Okay. This may take a few minutes," she sighed. "Could you possibly get us some wine?"

"No problem."

The walls that had once separated the loft into a variety of rooms had been removed. Screens and curtains had been hung to create smaller areas, but not lose the spacious open feeling. At one end there was organized singing and dancing. In another corner a demonstration of fighting techniques. Any number of groups were just standing and talking about everything from the Fair to current politics to the latest fantasy movie.

That was when he heard *the voice*. He had heard it only once before, on Hannah's answering machine, but it was something he could not forget. Standing a dozen feet from him was the tall, square, blondish figure whose face matched the Polaroid photo in Ashe's suitcase; the one he had found in the same house as the medieval fair flyer.

The man was a killer. The F.B.I. and a dozen different local police organizations had files on him, by deed but not by name. Eight killings were to his credit, with another four suspected, all in and around medieval and renaissance fairs. Ashe had no doubt that there were F.B.I. agents prowling the Fair. He also had no doubt that they would not discover him in a million years, unless he was presented to them on a silver platter.

"I tell you, m'lords and ladies, we are living in the ass end of history, in the dregs. Society today knows nothing, I say again *nothing*, of the concepts of honor and pride. In older, better times men understood things like that. They were ready to die for honor.

"We saw that today, when one of our own was attacked by a clod who knew nothing of honor, truth or justice. All this scum wanted was a chance to get into the pants of a woman. Then he did not even have the heart to stand and fight himself, he let a woman do it for him!"

The crowds around the man laughed. Ashe had seen these people before, with a hundred different faces in a hundred different places. They courted what seemed new and daring; the minute it bored them they were gone.

"So there you are!" Serina came up behind him, smiling, with two glasses of wine in her hand. "I had the feeling that you would never find the wine. I was wondering where you had run off to. I hoped I wouldn't find you in the arms of some ravishing wench, because I would have had to cut her tits off if I had."

"I would never risk your wrath, m'lady. Besides, why should I settle for second best when I am with the best," he said. "No, I was just listening to this fellow discoursing on what a terrible age we live in."

Serina looked over toward the crowd. The look on her face told Ashe that she knew the man. "I was hoping *he* wouldn't be here tonight. Though I can't honestly say I'm surprised. He blew into town a couple of months ago and has been trying to wrap the entire barony around his little finger. He disgusts me. Michael and he have become best buddies. Sometimes I think that they're attached at the hip, or maybe in some other organ of the body."

"What's his name?"

"Chalker. Ian Chalker. He sometimes uses the medieval name of Rudolph von Tarquin.

"But we're here to have a good time. Come on, there are some people I want to show you off to."

"Your wish is my command."

ASHE waited in the parking lot. He had left Serina talking to several other ladies, which suited him just fine. What he needed to do now, he needed to do without her.

Holding himself in the shadows, he watched as the square shaped figure of Chalker came closer. The sounds of the party drifted out open windows, voices and music blending together like a steady heartbeat.

Chalker had a half empty bottle of champagne in one hand, his car keys in the other. Ashe waited until the man had stopped in front of a station wagon. That was when he came out of the darkness, grabbing Chalker and slamming him hard against the car.

Keys and champagne bottle crashed to the ground. Then he pulled Chalker around, to face him. Ashe's hand, now holding a dagger, pushed the edge against Chalker's throat.

"Move and you're dead! Speak without my permission and you're dead! At this moment you may thank whatever dark gods watch over you that I'm allowing you to continue to breathe, even for a little while. Do you understand?" Ashe said.

Chalker nodded.

"Now listen and listen well. I know who you are and I know what you've done. Call yourself Ian Chalker, call yourself Groucho Marx or Stephen King. Call yourself any damn thing you want. I don't care! *I know who you really are!*"

"What are you?" whispered Chalker.

Ashe drove his fist hard into Chalker's stomach. "I told you not to speak unless I said you could. I don't do second chances. You've had your one strike. Next time I will be ripping your lungs out through your ears.

"But I will answer your question. I am fear. I am death. I am everything that you've ever seen when you stared into a woman's face, every bit of pain and terror you've pulled out of all those dead girls over the years. Now, I think it's time you say something in your own defense. If you can even have the gall to try and have one," Ashe said.

"I don't know what you're talking about," Chalker said. "You're insane. If it's money you want, take it. Take the car. My watch is a Rolex. That will get you at least a grand from a fence. Just take them and be gone."

Ashe shook his head. "I don't want your money. I don't want your watch; it's as phony as you are. I've come for your life. That's all that I want. In case it interests you, I'm the one who you were talking about earlier. I'm the one you said had no honor, no sense of pride. My pride and my blood have led me to you. Your friend Michael got the beating he deserved, from the woman he had mistreated. I'm here to give you something of the same."

"Then you're street scum, nothing but the lowest form of trash, you have no idea of how a true man fights his battles, otherwise you wouldn't have ambushed me from behind." Chalker said.

Ashe laughed as he watched. The man was swelling up with pride. It was the same bravado he had seen earlier in the middle of the crowd.

"One does what one has to. You don't know who it is you are

bandying words with about honor and heart, punk. I have forgotten more about true warriors and what it means to fight for honor than you have ever known," said Ashe.

"I'm sure that you know all about honor."

Ashe could feel his fangs sliding into place. The beast within him was struggling to get out. In his minds eye he could see himself ripping Chalker's throat to bloody shreds. The image, overlaid one of Hannah, as he had found her that night four months ago, carved into bloody pieces, her skin carefully removed and laid neatly on a white bridal bed.

"I'm going to give you more of a chance than you deserve."

With his last word, Ashe vanished. Chalker sagged back against his car, his breath coming in ragged gasps.

Then Ashe was there again, his form coalescing out of mist, standing only a few inches in front of Chalker.

"Owen Stadium in one hour. If you are a man of honor as you claim, a man better than this decadent age we live in, be there, with your sharpest sword. If you are not, I will hunt you down like the dog that you are and not give you the mercy I would a dumb animal."

Then Ashe was gone.

AN almost tomb-like silence filled Owen Stadium. As Ashe walked along the sidelines he knew that not a hundred yards away, beyond the southern wall of the stadium, cars were filling up Norman's main drag the sounds of their engines like a distant buzz of insects. Here there was only silence, and memories.

Football stadiums had always reminded Ashe of the old Roman arenas in Britain and France. The ones close to his family's ancestral holdings had been in ruins, but those near Camelot had been almost intact. The game itself was just another version of cavalry maneuvers, all the players needed were horses and sabers.

He remembered the long debates with Arthur about refurbishing the arenas. Arthur had wanted them left abandoned, remnants of a pagan past, but Ashe, or Lancelot du Lac, as he had been known then, had proclaimed them perfect for cavalry training. In the end he had won that argument and given Arthur the best mobile infantry of the time.

From a custom made case in the back of his van had come a broadsword. It had been designed just for him, made of the finest Toledo steel, the blade was razor sharp, the edge honed with infinite patience and practice.

The weapon was hidden by a long overcoat that Ashe carried over his arm. The local police would not be happy if, even during Medieval Fair, someone were caught carrying a sword, especially one like this, away from the event site.

Suggesting that they return to Serina's apartment, Ashe had left her there, asleep, with the implanted idea of a night full of passion to come. He spotted Chalker standing to one side of the home team's bench.

Ashe had discarded his medieval clothing, exchanging them for a black tee shit, jeans and a biker's leather jacket. Chalker, on the other hand, had gone to the opposite extreme. He now wore a full shirt of chain mail and a tabard emblazoned with a heraldic house badge; a helmet held under one arm and a fearsome looking sword resting on the ground.

"I wondered if you would show up," said Chalker.

"Really?" Ashe chuckled. "Since I issued the challenge, you doubted I would be here? That's muddy thinking; gets you in trouble every time."

"Honorless scum such as you have been known to lose their nerve."

"Honor? "

"I should expect someone like you to know little of honor and to disparage an honorable warrior. It is honor that will guide my blade in a fight," said Chalker.

"Speaking of fighting," said Ashe. "Did you come here to fight or to stand here chattering like a magpie all night. I noticed at the party that you seemed very adept at that latter skill."

The fury in Chalker's eyes blazed as he pulled the helmet over his head. Ashe dropped his jacket and unsheathed his sword.

"I suppose you know you won't walk out of here alive. But before we begin, tell me one thing," said Chalker. "I've never laid eyes on you before tonight. So why?"

"Why? Why do I want your life? Because you are a no good murdering piece of shit that persists in trying to act human. I make no claims to being human myself, but you, sir, are scum. Does the name Hannah Cortez mean anything to you?"

Chalker looked puzzled. "No. Should it?"

Ashe shook his head. "Cleveland. Four months ago. She was tall, with long brown hair, emerald eyes and an enjoyment of life like none I have ever seen. You should remember her. You should remember them all. You killed her, slowly, painfully."

Chalker grinned. He had sensed an advantage and meant to press it. "Oh, yes. Cleveland. Now I seem to recall her. I made her last for four days. Did you realize that she begged me to kill her? But I did it very slowly, very slowly. I made her last and savored each scream.

"You know, it's an art form. I did her a great honor taking her. She was one of the whores, you know. One of the ones that it is my holy charge to ride the world of!"

At that Chalker pulled his sword up and went for Ashe. Turning to one side Ashe let the other mans blade pass inches away from its target. Chalker whirled and struck again, this time Ashe deflected the blow by pushing his blade hard forward.

That his opponent had experience with a sword was obvious. He knew how to land a blow and to counter more than a few moves. Ashe let himself wait, attacking a few times, mostly to learn, to see how Chalker would react. Ashe himself had not stood to blood combat with a sword in nearly five years. There had been no call. But old skills, learned first in the practice fields of France, honed as one of Arthur's commanders and then used over the centuries, had not faded.

Sparks flew with each blow, showering each man in an otherworldly light. Ashe had begun to carefully drive Chalker back when the last thing in the world he expected happened.

Someone fired a shot.

The bullet came from behind Ashe, echoing like a backfiring truck among the empty seats of the stadium. Ashe swung wide and away from Chalker, turning as he moved back toward the stands. The gunman was making no attempt to hide himself. Standing just behind the metal railing at the fifty yard line was a the same figure he had seen that afternoon, dressed in a black and white musketeer's outfit. Michael, Serina's ex-boyfriend, his hands wrapped around the butt of a very large gun.

The second shot struck the turf not a foot from where Ashe stood.

"Looks like if I don't get you," laughed Chalker. "He will."

"Some man of honor you turned out to be, having your lackey ambush me!" said Ashe.

"One does what one can," said Chalker.

"I told you to stay away from her. Serina is mine. She will never belong to anyone else," Michael shouted. "I told you! I saw the two of you together, there in her bed rutting like animals! I warned you! Now you're going to pay."

Michael drew the gun up, assuming a firing stance, but before he could fire he suddenly lurched forward, crashing into the railing, the gun flying free from his hand to crash onto the fifty-yard line below him.

Standing behind him was Serina, a long wooden pole in her hand.

"I told you I'm not your girl friend any more!" Michael managed to stay on his feet, turning toward Serina. She produced a can of pepper gas and sprayed him directly in the eyes. That sent him screaming to the ground.

Ashe turned just as Chalker charged him. He managed to bring his sword up at the last moment, blocking the edge of the other man's blade as it sliced hard toward Ashe.

"You have no chance against me," Chalker's muffled voice said. "My skill has been honed for lifetimes, generations beyond anything that you can do."

"Indeed?" Ashe said.

Chalker struck at him three times in succession, slicing into the leather that wrapped around Ashe's arm.

"Indeed. My soul is an old one. Once I wore the name of Galahad of Camelot! I learned from the masters: Gawain, Arthur and even Lancelot himself!"

Ashe laughed. The very thought that this "man" could be carrying the soul of Galahad was a repugnant one. He struck hard against Chalker, his sword cutting into the chain mail the man wore.

"You are not Galahad. If your soul were his, he would have killed himself before allowing you to do the things that you have done. I knew Galahad. Galahad was a friend of mine. You're no Galahad!"

"What would you know? You're nothing but street scum, not even fit to clean the stables of Camelot."

"I? I am Lancelot!" With those words Ashe drove his sword down hard pushing aside the other man's blade, his weapon cutting deep into chain mail and then flesh of the Chalker's stomach. His foe stood there, staring, uncomprehending. Ashe pulled his blade clear and then drove it into Chalker's neck. The bone and flesh clung together for only a moment, then cut through. The head lingered where it was for a few seconds, teetering from side to side, before rolling from his shoulders; blood washing it and the green turf.

With a single movement Ashe kicked the head straight between the goal posts.

"He scores, and the crowd goes wild," he said.

"I hope you take this in the right way," Ashe said. "Understand, I am grateful as all hell, but I would like to know just what you were doing there? I expected you to be sound asleep until morning."

Serina laughed. "You're welcome. You should learn to never take anything for granted."

They had left the stadium quickly, retrieving Serina's bicycle and then heading for an alley near the student union where Ashe had parked his van.

"My place," she said.

"Okay, but I'm still waiting for an answer," he said.

"And I'm still waiting for my stomach to stop churning. It isn't often that I see somebody decapitated," she said.

Ashe could understand her reaction. Even through the dim mists of centuries, he could recall the first time that he had ridden to battle with his father's army. His reaction after the fighting was over had been anything but heroic. The sight of Lancelot du Lac throwing up was not one that fit the legend that had come to be associated with the name. But then again, Ashe had never felt like he wanted to fit *that* image anyway.

"I heard what he said to you," she said slowly. "About killing all those women. Was it true?"

"I only wish it weren't. " He wasn't sure if the police would be able to connect Chalker with the killings or if this would be listed as some bizarre gang execution.

"And what about Michael?"

"Oh, him?" grinned Ashe. "I don't think we'll have to worry about a thing with Michael."

Ashe had roused Michael and then carefully *suggested* to him that he had not seen any one of them that night. Instead, Michael had gone out after the medieval party and gotten plastered, failed miserably when he tried to pick up a couple of coeds, then headed for his own home to sleep it off. If any of the memories ever returned to him it would be in the form of nightmares that would make no sense to him.

"Normally, when I implant a suggestion in someone's mind, they do what I require of them." Ashe had now and again encountered those who were immune to his abilities. Thankfully this had been one of those times.

Serina grinned. "You guys think that all you have to do is snap a finger and a girl is in your power. Hello! I've got news for you. I've never been that easy to hypnotize. When you tried to do it I decided to follow you and see if I could find out what was going on. Just consider yourself lucky that I did."

"Oh, that I do, m'lady."

"Now, just on the off chance that the police question you about Chalker's death," said Serina. "Just tell them that you spent the entire night with me. Besides, you didn't think that I was through with you? Did you?"

"I wouldn't think of being that presumptuous."

"Of course not."

ABOUT THE AUTHOR

Not too long ago a friend of Brad's said that he wrote family stories. Brad replied, "Yeah, if you are talking about The Addams Family or relatives of Dracula."

Brad's short fiction has appeared in the MEROVINGEN NIGHTS series, TIME OF THE VAMPIRES, ON CRUSADE: More Tales Of the Knights Templar, LORD OF THE FANTASTIC: Stories in Tribute to Roger Zelazny, HORRORS: 365 Scary Stories, MERLIN, SUCH A PRETTY FACE, WARRIOR FANTASTIC, SINGLE WHITE VAMPIRE, DRACULA IN LONDON, KNIGHT FANTASTIC and other places including the two Yard Dog Press anthologies mentioned in the following pages. Five of his stories were recently published in the chapbook DARK AND STORMY NIGHTS. More of his fiction will be appearing in THE MAGIC SHOP and MEN WRITING SF AS WOMEN anthologies in the near future.

His nonfiction has turned up in such diverse venues as PER SONAL DEMONS, STARLOG, STAR TREK THE NEXT GENERATION magazine, BABY BOOMER COLLECTIBLES, DARK ZONES, WEIRD TALES, CALIFORNIA HIGHWAY PATROLMAN magazine, PERSIMMON HILL and others.

ABOUT THE COVER ARTIST

Tania Mears is an accomplished photographer who usually works more mundane venues like weddings and family reunions. This is her second cover shot for YDP; the first was for the cover of THE FOLLY OF ASSUMPTION by Lee Martindale (which is no longer in print).

Tania lives with her husband Mark in Fort Smith, Arkansas. Her hobbies include writing poetry, acting in her local theater group, and gardening.

Tania has been with Yard Dog Press from the beginning when she created the character Raje and wrote her dialogue for the comic strip in *Yard Dog Comic Magazine*. Raje appeared as a separate strip for several issues, then the character became part of the on-going saga of the "Torque City Blues." She also co-wrote the strip "Yard Dog Willie and Splotch."

Yard Dog Press Titles As Of This Print Date

The Green Women, Laura J. Underwood
The Guardians, Lynn Abbey
Hammer Town, Selina Rosen
The Happiness Box, Beverly A. Hale
The Host Series: The Host, Fright Eater, Gang Approval, Selina
    Rosen
Houston, We've Got Bubbas!, Edited by Selina Rosen
How I Spent the Apocolypse, Selina Rosen
I Didn't Quite Make It To Oz, Edited by Selina Rosen
I Should Have Stayed In Oz, Edited by Selina Rosen
In the Shadows, Bradley H. Sinor
International House of Bubbas, Edited by Selina Rosen
It's the Great Bumpkin, Cletus Brown!, Katherine A. Turski
The Killswitch Review, Steven-Elliot Altman & Diane DeKelb-
    Rittenhouse
The Leopard's Daughter, Lee Killough
The Lightning Horse, John Moore
The Logic of Departure, Mark W. Tiedemann
The Long, Cold Walk To Mars, Jeffrey Turner
Marking the Signs and Other Tales Of Mischief, Laura J. Underwood
Material Things, Selina Rosen
Medieval Misfits: Renaissance Rejects, Tracy S. Morris
Mirror Images, Susan Satterfield
Mirror, Mirror and Other Reflections, James K. Burk
More Stories That Won't Make Your Parents Hurl, Edited by Selina
    Rosen
Music for Four Hands, Louis Antonelli & Edward Morris
My Life with Geeks and Freaks, Claudia Christian
The Necronomicrap: A Guide To Your Horooooscope, Tim Frayser
Playing With Secrets, Bradley H & Sue P. Sinor
Redheads In Love, Linda L. Donahue, Rhonda Eudaly, Julia S.
    Mandala, & Dusty Rainbolt
Reruns, Selina Rosen
Rock 'n' Roll Universe, Ken Rand
Shadows In Green, Richard Dansky
Stories That Won't Make Your Parents Hurl, Edited by Selina Rosen
Tales from Keltora, Laura J. Underwood
*Tales Of the Lucky Nickel Saloon, Second Ave., Laramie, Wyoming, U
    S of A*, Ken Rand
Tarbox Station, Rhonda Eudaly
Texistani: Indo-Pak Food From A Texas Kitchen, Beverly A. Hale
That's All Folks, J. F. Gonzalez
Through Wyoming Eyes, Ken Rand
Turn Left to Tomorrow, Robin Wayne Bailey
The Twins, Selina Rosen
Wandering Lark, Laura J. Underwood

Wings of Morning, Katharine Eliska Kimbriel
Zombies In Oz and Other Undead Musings, Robin Wayne Bailey

Double Dog
(A YDP Imprint):

#1:
Of Stars & Shadows, Mark W.
Tiedemann
This Instance Of Me, Jeffrey Turner

#2:
Gods and Other Children, Bill D. Allen
Tranquility, Tracy Morris

#3:
Home Is the Hunter, James K. Burk
Farstep Station, Lazette Gifford

#4:
Sabre Dance, Melanie Fletcher
The Lunari Mask, Laura J. Underwood

#5:
House of Doors, Julia Mandala
Jaguar Moon, Linda A. Donahue

Just Cause
(A YDP Imprint):

The Bitter End
Selina Rosen

Death Under the Crescent Moon
Dusty Rainbolt

The Ghost Writer
Selina Rosen

It's Not Rocket Science: Spirituality for the Working-Class Soul
Selina Rosen

Meditations of a Hoarder
Melinda LaFevers

Not My Life
Selina Rosen

The Pit
Selina Rosen

Plots and Protagonists: A Reference Guide for Writers
Mel. White

Vanishing Fame
Selina Rosen

Non-YDP titles we distribute:

Chains of Freedom
Chains of Destruction
Jabone's Sword
Queen of Denial
Recycled
Strange Robby
Sword Masters
Selina Rosen

Three Ways to Order:

1. Write us a letter telling us what you want, then send it along with your check or money order (made payable to Yard Dog Press) to: Yard Dog Press, 710 W. Redbud Lane, Alma, AR 72921-7247

2. Use selinarosen@cox.net or lynnstran@cox.net to contact us and place your order. Then send your check or money order to the address above. *This has the advantage of allowing you to check on the availability of short-stock items such as T-shirts and back-issues of Yard Dog Comics.*

3. Contact us as in #1 or #2 above and pay with a credit card or by debit from your checking account. Either give us the credit card information in your letter/Email/phone call, or go to our website and use our shopping carts. If you send us your information, please include your name as it appears on the card, your credit card number, the expiration date, and the 3 or 4-digit security code after your signature on the back (CVV). Please remember that we will include media rate (minimum $3.00) S/H for mailing in the lower 48 states.

Watch our website at
www.yarddogpress.com
for news of upcoming projects
and new titles!!

A Note to Our Readers

We at Yard Dog Press understand that many people buy used books because they simply can't afford new ones. That said, and understanding that not everyone is made of money, we'd like you to know something that you may not have realized. Writers only make money on new books that sell. At the big houses a writer's entire future can hinge on the number of books they sell. While this isn't the case at Yard Dog Press, the honest truth is that when you sell or trade your book or let many people read it, the writer and the publishing house aren't making any money.

As much as we'd all like to believe that we can exist on love and sweet potato pie, the truth is we all need money to buy the things essential to our daily lives. Writers and publishers are no different.

We realize that these "freebies" and cheap books often turn people on to new writers and books that they wouldn't otherwise read. However we hope that you will reconsider selling your copy, and that if you trade it or let your friends borrow it, you also pass on the information that if they really like the author's work they should consider buying one of their books at full price sometime so that the writer can afford to continue to write work that entertains you.

We appreciate all our readers and *depend* upon their support.

Thanks,
The Editorial Staff
Yard Dog Press

PS – Please note that "used" books without covers have, in most cases, been stolen. Neither the author nor the publisher has made any money on these books because they were supposed to be pulped for lack of sales.

Please do not purchase books without covers.

www.ingramcontent.com/pod-product-compliance
Lightning Source LLC
Chambersburg PA
CBHW030514130626
46549CB00007B/2989